THE CINDERELLA SUBSTITUTE

In the two years since the tragic car crash that killed his fiancée, Nate Mayer has successfully avoided another relationship. His family, and especially his twin sister, Nathalie are worried. Jennifer Blake is Nate's personal assistant. Hired after the accident, she has her own problems to deal with, including the deaths of her adoptive parents and the debts incurred by their nursing care. But those difficulties pale into insignificance when Jenni finally traces her birth mother...

THE CINDERELLA
SUBSTITUTE

The Cinderella Substitute

by

Nell Dixon

Magna Large Print Books
Long Preston, North Yorkshire,
BD23 4ND, England.

ISBN 978-0-7505-3663-9

Copyright © 2006 Nell Dixon

Cover illustration © Ilona Wellmann by arrangement with
Arcangel Images

The moral right of the author has been asserted

Published in Large Print 2013 by arrangement with
Nell Dixon

Magna Large Print is an imprint of Library Magna Books Ltd.

Printed and bound in Great Britain by
T.J. (International) Ltd., Cornwall, PL28 8RW

For David who always believed in me and Jessica Foote, without whom this book would never have seen the light of day.

CHAPTER ONE

Nate jabbed the buzzer on his desk for the third time. *Where on earth was Jenni?* He paced up and down the room, glaring at the closed office door.

What could be keeping her? Today of all days he needed to get going, finish up the job in hand and escape. Away from the sympathetic glances of his employees and the murmured conversations which stopped abruptly whenever he came within earshot.

He opened the door to her office and saw her in her usual seat behind the curved ash desk. *So why hadn't she answered the buzzer?* He crossed the pale green carpet in a couple of paces. As he got closer to her, he knew something was wrong. Her back was towards him and her shoulders quivered.

'Jenni?'

He moved round the desk to take a better look. A pile of post lay unopened in front of her, one envelope still secured in her slim fingers.

'What's the matter? Are you ill?'

Nate couldn't imagine why his super-efficient personal secretary appeared to be having some kind of breakdown. Jenni never broke down. She had insisted on returning to work after only a few days' leave after her adoptive mother died.

She shook her head and he caught a glimpse of tears on her pale face. For a split second he wondered if Jenni had developed some kind of sympathy scenario for him based on the office rumour mill. He dismissed that idea as quickly as it had arisen. One of his main reasons for employing Jenni had been her complete lack of interest in gossip and speculation.

'I'm all right.' She wiped the tears away from under her glasses with shaking fingers.

Nate sighed. 'Well you don't look it,' he remarked. In fact, now he came to think of it, Jenni looked positively unwell.

'You're not doing one of those faddy diets?' He hoped he'd hit on the right answer. It had to be something like that.

She blinked with astonishment and glared at him. 'No!'

Nate settled back onto the edge of her desk and folded his arms. He'd have to think again now his first theory had been shot out of the water.

'Good. You're skinny enough. In fact,' he ran a critical eye over her appearance, '–too skinny.' He thought she'd lost a lot of weight, diet or no diet. Her black office suit looked baggy and her small face had a pinched expression.

He felt a momentary pang of guilt *How come he hadn't noticed?* He spent more time with Jenni than with any other living creature, except Rufus, his chocolate Labrador. Inspiration hit as he considered the many late nights and weekends Jenni had put in at the company over the last few weeks.

'Boyfriend trouble?' he suggested, confident that he'd managed to solve the puzzle.

'Nate!' The colour returned to her pale face and her expression assumed the cool blank look she reserved for the most irritating of their clients.

'So do I get an explanation?' He tapped his foot against the side of the desk as he waited for a response.

'I'm not sure that you do, to be honest,' she said, sounding icy. At least she appeared to be returning to her normal, sensible, practical self.

He made a mental note to be more considerate of her social life in future when he asked her to do overtime. Just because work saved him from being alone with his thoughts didn't mean Jenni deserved the same.

'Maybe I'd better deal with the rest of the post and then we can get some work done today.' He reached over to take the pile of letters from her lap.

'No!' Her quick snatch took him by surprise. 'Erm, that is, I mean...' She extracted the letter that had been uppermost in the pile. 'Here you are.' She passed the remainder over to him.

'Jenni, what's going on?' Her strange behaviour bothered him.

She hesitated. 'I got a letter from my mother.'

For a moment he questioned her sanity. Dead people didn't write letters. Then it clicked. 'Your birth mother?'

'Remember I asked if it would be all right to use the office address because you said not to use my own?'

It came back to him then, a late night conversation after work when Jenni had asked his advice about contacting her real mother.

'She wrote back to you?'

'I sent a letter with a self-addressed envelope. I thought it would make her more likely to respond.' Her hands trembled as she smoothed the envelope. 'I recognised it when I fetched the mail.'

'You haven't opened it.'

She licked her lips and with a desultory shrug of her shoulders said, 'I was scared. What if she doesn't want to know me?'

An overwhelming rush of pity surged through Nate. He knew from little things she had mentioned that she'd had a tough life, and she had been on her own since her adoptive parents had died.

'Do you want me to open it?' He made the offer before he had time to think.

'I...' She hovered for a moment, and then pushed the envelope towards him. 'Okay.'

He ripped it open and thought at first the woman had merely mailed back Jenni's original letter. Then, as he flipped it over, he saw the short note scribbled on the back in unformed child-like scrawl.

'What's the matter? What does it say?' Jenni's slender frame trembled and her face paled even further.

He spoke quickly to reassure her. 'It's all right. She wants to meet you.' He passed the letter over.

Jenni read it through, then glanced up at him with a worried expression. 'Tomorrow. She wants to meet me tomorrow.'

'Do you know the café she's talking about?' Nate was deeply concerned. The hasty scrawl didn't smack of a mother desperate to make a good impression on a daughter she hadn't seen in years.

'I think so. It's on the other side of town. Near where the new ring road is being built.' She still looked shell-shocked as she studied her mother's handwriting as if it would yield some hidden message.

He knew the area she meant. The buildings appeared run-down and gangs of youths hung around on the street corners. Many of the shops had been boarded over as once thriving businesses had closed down.

'I'm coming with you tomorrow.' He noted Jenni looked stunned rather than grateful.

'That's very kind of you, Nate, but I'll be fine,' she stammered. 'It's nice of you to offer though.'

'It wasn't a suggestion, Jen. I'm coming with you. It's a bad area. There have been a lot of muggings around that part of town.' He couldn't let her go on her own.

'It's Saturday tomorrow, Nate. You can't give up your day off just for me.' A pretty pink flush tinted her cheekbones and her eyes shone. Jenni had nice eyes. Very nice eyes. What was the matter with him today? He'd seen Jenni's eyes a thousand times before, hadn't he?

'Really, it's no big deal. I haven't anything planned and you've done me loads of favours. Think of it as me paying you back a little.' He shuffled uneasily on the hard edge of the desk while Jenni continued to study his face.

She smiled at him, taking him by surprise.

'Well thanks anyway, Nate. It's really nice of you and I do appreciate it.

After Nate had departed to his own office, Jenni stashed her precious letter away inside her handbag, and made sure the fastener of the inner pocket was locked shut.

Why had she become so emotional over that letter? Nate must think she was such an idiot. Still, it was hard not to feel rattled when he had sat himself in front of her like a big brooding colossus! Interrogating her on her diet and her love life! *What love life?* asked the little voice in her brain. *The only guy who's interested in you is the Fed Ex man and he must be fifty!*

Jenni sighed as she crossed the room to switch the coffee machine on. She twitched her skirt back into position. She *had* lost weight. The stupid thing had twisted around on her again. Maybe she should do as her friend Lorna suggested and break into her precious savings for a new outfit.

The phone on her desk rang, making her switch her mind back on to work as she walked over to answer it. Jenni felt sure Nate wasn't in the mood today for his twin sister's well-intentioned concern as she transferred the call to his phone. Nathalie often called the office as she appeared to be close to her brother, but today wasn't any ordinary day.

Sure enough, a few minutes later the door of his office flew open. He stalked out, pulling on his jacket as he walked.

'Jenni, get your coat! We're going on a site visit.'

She grabbed her handbag ready to shove her notebook and Dictaphone into the side pocket. 'Where are we going?'

'River Park. Anywhere, as long as I'm away from interfering...' he broke off, still muttering.

She pulled her coat on hurriedly and followed as he strode down the cream walled corridor to the lift.

Only when they were several miles away from the office did Nate appear to relax. Jenni ventured a cautious peek. His shoulders had slumped and although his mouth was still set, the lines of his face appeared less harsh.

A pang of sadness pierced her heart. He must have loved Cerys very much. Two years had passed since the accident and he still grieved. Wistfully she allowed herself the luxury of wondering what it must be like to be loved so much.

The car slowed and stopped at traffic lights. Jenni noticed the name on the street opposite.

'That's the Café!' The words jolted out of her mouth before she had time to think.

It wasn't a cosy tearoom with chintz-covered tables. Layers of road dirt partly obscured the glass window at the front and a cracked, gaudy neon sign hung above the door. Inside the gloomy interior, Jenni could just see the fat red and yellow plastic condiment containers on the brown table tops.

'That's where your mother wants to meet you?' Nate's voice was curiously gentle. Jenni blinked back tears for the second time in one day.

'Afraid so.' To her dismay, her voice sounded brittle. She was relieved when the lights changed and the car moved forward.

She tried to picture herself and Nate

19

entering the grubby little café, but failed miserably. If she were on her own maybe no one would notice her, but with Nate? She fiddled with the leather strap of her wristwatch. She had never seen Nate in anything other than the smart designer suits he wore for work. Nate and that miserable café were like chalk and cheese. Her brain began to race around, and she started to panic.

His inner radar must have detected her doubts.

'It'll be all right Jen.' He sounded so sure that she couldn't help betraying her surprise.

'It just doesn't seem like the kind of venue that would entice someone to give up a hard-earned Saturday afternoon off,' she said apologetically.

'It also doesn't seem like the kind of place you would be safe to go to and meet a stranger on your own.' Nate's tone suggested he wasn't prepared to argue the matter any further.

They pulled up in one of the newly completed car parks outside the River Park shopping centre. The gleaming new building was almost finished. Retailers had already moved in, no doubt hoping to catch some of the Christmas trade. Minor glitches had delayed the final finish. Jenni knew Nate was determined to prevent any extension on the contract, which might cost the company money in time penalties.

Nate called the site foreman on his mobile to let him know they were there as they entered through the automatic doors. The transformation that had taken place since their last visit amazed her. Mr Doughty, the foreman, came to meet them and took them to the problem area near the lifts. A bluff man in his fifties, he always managed to irritate Jenni whenever they met by referring to her as 'the little lassie.'

A short tour of inspection and a flurry of phone calls later, Mr Doughty escorted them back to the entrance.

'I dare say you'll be glad to get back to your office today. The little lassie looks a bit peaky,' he said jovially.

Jenni shivered as they headed back to the car. Nate frowned at her, his face concerned.

'I think Mr Doughty has a point. You look awful, Jen.'

'Well, thank you! You sure know how to make a girl feel good. I've told you I'm fine. It's just chilly out here after being inside.'

Nate raised one dark eyebrow at her uncharacteristic outburst.

She pushed her glasses back onto the bridge of her nose and looked at him, daring him to contradict her. Nate was a nice guy but there were times when a few lessons in tact wouldn't go amiss.

'Okay, I'm not going to argue with you.' He unlocked the car.

'It's almost lunchtime. Do you want me to get sandwiches?' She fastened her seatbelt, ready for the trip back to the office.

'And when did you last fetch yourself a sandwich?' he accused. 'Now I come to think of it, I only ever see you drinking those disgusting packet soups.'

Her cheeks heated with a guilty flush. The truth was she couldn't afford to buy lunch very often. Not because Nate didn't pay her well, he did. But it was cheaper to bring food from home while she struggled to pay off the debts incurred by her adoptive mother's illness.

She noticed they weren't heading back towards the city. 'Where are we going?'

'To get lunch,' he said shortly.

She did a rapid mental calculation of how much money she had in her purse. 'I haven't enough money with me to buy out today!'

He threw her a look of amazement. 'I'm buying. Consider it part of the payback. I think we both could use a break.'

The road they ended up on narrowed into a single lane track. Bare twigs from the hedgerow brushed against the sides of the Range Rover as they made their way towards a white building up ahead. A thin plume of smoke wisped from the chimney into an ominous grey sky.

Jenni felt unusually nervous as Nate helped her down the high step of the Range Rover. She had been out for working lunches before with him, but there had been clients or other staff with them on those occasions.

The light pressure of his fingers on her gloved hand disturbed her senses making her tingle all over.

'Are you sure you're well, Jen?' He gave her a puzzled look.

'Fine.' She found the lie tripped off her tongue, well aware he hadn't shared the sensation with her.

He led the way into the pub. The landlord called to him in recognition and Jenni guessed he'd visited many times before.

As she sat down and slipped off her coat and gloves, Nate ordered her a steaming mug of hot chocolate, which appeared with remarkable speed, along with his order for coffee.

'I thought it would warm you up,' he said, when she gave him a questioning glance. 'It's much colder outside now and you look so pale today.'

Jenni suppressed a sigh. That would teach her to skimp on make-up.

The menu arrived and she studied it with care. A hot meal would be wonderful. She'd eaten too many economy dinners over the last few months.

'Choose what you want, Jen.' Blushing, she realised he'd misinterpreted her hesitation over ordering.

'I'd like the steak and kidney pudding, please.'

He smiled at her in approval and asked for the same dish for himself.

She sipped her drink while she relished the warmth from the fire. The interior of the bar fascinated her and she gazed around with curiosity. She'd never been in many pubs. Her father had always condemned them as places of iniquity filled with loose women. A little frisson of guilty pleasure nibbled at her conscience.

'I come here with Rufus after I've walked him down by the river at weekends,' Nate said.

She looked at the oak beams and the tasteful decorations surrounding the bar. A large Christmas tree twinkled in the corner and the scent of pine needles mingled with the wood smoke of the fire.

'It's nice,' she said and meant it. It *was* nice, nice to escape for a little while and to sit somewhere warm and cosy. It was nice to eat a lovely filling meal which had been cooked for her and to have pleasant, congenial company while she did so.

'It's been a strange day today.' She spoke without thinking. His expression altered and she added, 'I mean, hearing from my birth mother. I wonder what she's like.' Jenni noticed him relax again and cursed herself for forgetting about the day's significance for Nate.

'Well, I guess we'll find out tomorrow.' His dark blue eyes seared into her. 'Just don't get your hopes up too high, Jen. Remember, you don't know anything about her.'

The meal arrived and saved her from answering. She *did* know about her, if her adoptive father was to be believed. He had certainly voiced his low opinion of her birth mother often enough – usually when pointing out Jenni's faults and comparing them to her unknown parent.

She shoved the memory away and began

to eat. The pie was good, crisp light pastry with a tasty steak filling. She had forgotten how good it felt to go out. It had been such a long time since she'd had a date. *Not that this is a date,* she thought.

'I guess you were hungry after all then?' Intent on her food, she hadn't noticed how quickly she'd been eating until Nate's comment. Embarrassed, she realised her plate appeared almost empty whilst he had yet to eat over half of his food.

Flustered, she didn't know what to say. Social situations always had the effect of making her feel inadequate.

'Relax, Jen, I was teasing you.' He smiled at her, obviously amused by her uncertainty.

Hesitantly, she smiled back. 'I suppose I was hungrier than I thought.'

He looked so different when he smiled – younger, and the shadows under his eyes lifted a little. *What was she doing?* Nate was her boss, her friend. *When had she ever noticed that he was good looking? With dark blue eyes framed by long black lashes, high cheekbones and a very nicely shaped, kissable...*

Shocked by her thoughts, she called a halt right there. Nate still loved Cerys and even if he were heart-free, she knew he wouldn't be interested in her.

Later on, feeling warmer and fuller, they emerged into the dull wintry afternoon.

'It's not worth going back to the office. We've put in enough extra hours there lately. I'll take you home.'

She guessed it wasn't his real reason for not wanting to return to work. He had been late arriving this morning, and she had surmised from his strained expression that he had probably visited Cerys' grave first.

'Well, if you're sure. You're the boss!' If she were honest with herself, she didn't feel like returning to work any more than he did. She'd worked herself up with worries about meeting her mother.

'What time do you want me to pick you up tomorrow?' He took the turn towards the rundown residential area where Jenni lived.

'Um, I thought maybe one o'clock. I'd like to be there a bit early.'

He nodded a reply while negotiating the car through a narrow side street.

'Where along here do you live?' He'd never been to her area before. Whenever she worked late he always called a cab for her.

'Over there.' She indicated the small parade of shop fronts with her gloved hand and he drew to a halt.

She could see him looking for her home.

As she viewed the street through his eyes, the unwelcome heat of a defensive flush built in her cheeks. A bigger contrast to the beautiful regency building where Nate lived would be hard to find.

'So where is your flat?'

The shop fronts looked scruffy and neglected in the gloomy wintry light. A chip shop, an off license, a post office, a hairdresser's and the bait and tackle shop which catered for the local fishermen sat sulking before them.

'I live above the hairdresser's. There's my door, by the post box.' She indicated a blue painted front door. 'I have a doorbell but I'll look out for your car,' she added. It would be too embarrassing to have Nate come up to her tiny flat.

Nate gave her a curious look and she knew he had to be wondering why she lived in such a horrible place when he paid her a more than generous wage. Still, she didn't plan to stay there forever, it was just until her debts were cleared. Then she could look for somewhere better and move on.

'Well, thanks again for lunch. It was really nice.' She released the seatbelt and hoped he wasn't expecting to be asked in for a drink.

'My pleasure. I'll see you tomorrow, Jen.'

She knew he must be thinking her rude, but she simply couldn't bear to invite him into her shabby flat with its second-hand furniture. The permanent smell of old chips lingered from the takeaway despite her best efforts with potpourri and scented candles.

The cold wind hit her face as she climbed out of the car. Nate leaned across to pull the door shut and she smelt the faint musky scent of his cologne.

'Get an early night and don't worry about tomorrow. Everything will be fine, you'll see.'

Jenni left the security of his presence behind and crossed the road. Alone once more, she could only hope he was right.

CHAPTER TWO

Nate woke with a cry. His heart raced, and drops of sweat beaded his body. He looked at his watch. Three-thirty a.m. He groaned to himself and scrubbed his hands through his hair, hoping the action would rouse him enough to remove the remnants of his nightmare.

He slid out of the clammy cotton sheets and headed for the bathroom. Nate splashed his face with cool water to clear his head. The nightmare of the crash had been particularly vivid, even more than usual. It brought with it the now familiar feelings of guilt and loss.

He debated the idea of making himself a drink and returning to bed, but he knew he wasn't going to go back to sleep for a while. There was only one sure-fire method he had found to cope. He pulled on a dressing gown as he walked slowly downstairs to the study, switched on the computer and prepared to lose himself in his work.

Jenni had spent a restless night. She had lain

awake till the early hours of the morning as she tossed and turned on the narrow mattress of her single bed, unable to ignore the different scenarios of meeting her mother, which crept into her mind. What would her mother look like? How would she recognize her? Was she doing the right thing in allowing Nate to tag along?

To her surprise the last question had robbed her of nearly as much sleep as any of the others.

She had always been aware of Nate's attractiveness, but because of his past – and her own – she had never allowed it to impact on her. She couldn't change her mind now.

She shook her head at her fancifulness, and concentrated on the other key problem – how to recognize her mother. Jenni knelt on the floor beside the bed and pulled out the battered grey metal box holding her most treasured possessions.

With a deep breath for courage, she pushed open the dented lid. Inside was her original birth certificate with the name her birth mother had given her – Chantelle.

Her adoptive father's voice rang in her head. *'What kind of name was that to give a child? Of course we had to change it. People would have got entirely the wrong impression.*

We chose Jennifer, after my mother. Much more respectable.'

She pushed the piece of paper carefully to one side and searched for the only photograph in her possession of the woman who had given birth to her. The indistinct blurry features smiled back at her, a woman younger than Jenni was now, dressed in the fashion of the day. Her mother, the woman who had called her Chantelle, and kept her for six months before giving her up for adoption.

After a shower, Jenni surveyed her wardrobe gloomily as she wondered what to wear. With a heavy sigh, she selected her smartest pair of jeans and the cornflower blue sweater Lorna had given her a few months ago as a birthday gift. She would have to buy some new clothes soon. She couldn't keep putting it off. The annual Christmas dance was only a few weeks away and she knew Nate wouldn't let her slide out of attending this year.

He had already roped her in to organize everything. She knew the rest of the employees looked forward to it. She found it difficult to picture Nate dressed as Santa Claus giving out gifts, but Lorna had assured her it was a company tradition.

The morning dragged by, although with the number of times Jenni checked her watch, it was hardly surprising.

The unexpected sound of the downstairs buzzer threw her into turmoil. It couldn't be Nate. If so, he'd come to fetch her far too early. She peered out of her lounge window only to see him standing on the pavement in front of the hairdressing salon.

As she opened the downstairs door to the cold wintry day, a figure holding a huge bunch of flowers unexpectedly confronted her.

'I took the liberty of bringing you these.' Nate sounded muffled from behind the dazzling bouquet of pink carnations, purple freesias and babies breath.

'Well, um... Thank you.' Jenni stammered with confusion. No one had *ever* given her flowers before.

'I don't suppose I could come in? It's rather cold out here.'

Mortified by her bad manners, she accepted the bouquet and ushered Nate inside. 'My flat is right up the stairs. Please sit down while I arrange these in some water.'

Flustered, she hunted in her tiny kitchen for a container. Eventually she found a tall white china milk jug that had escaped the auction of her adoptive parents' belongings. She filled it with water and did her best to arrange the flowers in the makeshift vase. She carried it back through to the lounge where she set the precarious arrangement on the windowsill.

Nate had removed his leather jacket and sat down on the corner of her old-fashioned, overstuffed settee. The small lounge appeared even smaller with Nate inside it. The corner of his mouth twitched as he gravely regarded her attempt at floristry, and her cheeks heated.

'Can I get you a drink of anything before we go? I think we've got time.' She looked at her watch for the millionth time that day to check.

'A cup of tea would be nice. At least I know you're better at that than you are at flower arranging,' he declared with a straight face as one of the carnations overbalanced and slid out of the jug.

'Oh, no!' Jenni dived to rescue it and restore it to the container, but giggles got the better of her and she decided to confess. 'I don't actually have a vase. The milk jug was the best thing I could find.' Her face burnt as she attempted to stuff the recalcitrant bloom back into the pot.

She scuttled into the kitchen before Nate could comment on her confession. Safe from view, she switched on the kettle and busied herself finding the mugs while she cooled down. Her lack of social skills bothered her as she'd never entertained anyone in her home before except Lorna.

With the tea made and feeling calmer, she carried the drinks back into the lounge and handed one to Nate. Jenni couldn't decipher his expression as he studied his surroundings. She'd done her best to make her room attractive; covering the sofas with colorful throws and hiding the ugly wallpaper with her artwork.

'Are the paintings your own work?'

Anxiety welled up inside Jenni as she watched him examine her pictures. She had never shown anyone except Loma her pictures. In fact, no one else even knew she painted.

'These are very good.' The genuine admiration in Nate's tone made her forget her diffidence for a moment.

'You really like them?' She had always done little pictures and sketches for her own pleasure but had learned as a child to keep it to herself, like so many other things.

'They're very good, Jenni. I didn't realize I had such a talented P.A.'

Aware she must have a smile like a Cheshire cat, she blushed. Nate always praised her work at the office, but this felt different. More personal.

He drained his mug then examined his watch. 'We ought to leave if you want to be there a little early.'

With a few quick gulps she swallowed the rest of her drink. Nate pulled on his coat ready to leave as she took both mugs into the kitchen. She picked up her coat and bag from the hook by the door and felt the nerves of her stomach rebel against the hot fluid she had so hastily deposited in there.

As she climbed into Nate's car, she saw him through new eyes. His long legs, encased in dark denim jeans, emphasized his muscular thighs. The dark grey sweater he wore under his black leather jacket served to enhance his brooding good looks.

She pushed her glasses back up to the bridge of her nose and mentally vowed to fix the loose screw in the frame. It was high time she either bought new ones or changed to contact lenses. Another one of the expenses she had been delaying.

Halfway to the café, an urge to stop the car

and run away swept through her. She couldn't decide which was worse: feeling so excited to be meeting her mother at last, or fear she might be making a terrible mistake and would end up getting hurt.

Nate parked the car a couple of streets away from the café. Jenni's legs shook as he helped her down from the car. However, the touch of his hand reassured her. He slipped his arm through hers, keeping it there as they made their way through the dingy back streets to the café.

The establishment appeared deserted, except for the sulky-faced teenage girl who half-heartedly filled sauce bottles at the counter. Jenni took a seat near the window so she could see anyone approach while Nate fetched them both cups of tea in pale green utility china cups.

'Do you have any idea what she looks like, Jenni?' he asked in a low voice on his return.

She reached inside her bag for the precious photograph. He studied it with care, looking first at the photo and then at Jenni.

'You have the same eyes.' He sounded thoughtful.

Jenni tucked the photograph back inside her bag, and continued to look hopefully through the grimy window at the empty

38

street outside.

Nate chatted amiably to while away the time – light, inconsequential conversation which made no demands of her. Time slipped away and the last vestiges of hope that her mother might still arrive died when Jenni realized the hands on Nate's watch had already slid round to three o'clock.

She blinked back the tears that threatened to brim behind her glasses, and gathered her bag, ready to leave.

'I'm sorry, Jenni.' Nate slipped his arm around her shoulder and gave her a gentle hug.

'Why do you think she didn't come?' Disappointment gave way to anger. The feelings of resentment from long ago stirred in her heart.

Nate shrugged. 'It could be anything, Jen. She might have had trouble getting away, a crisis at home or she simply might not have felt able to face you in the end. Maybe she was just scared.'

She knew he was probably right, but it didn't stop her feeling that it wasn't fair to have her hopes built up, only to have them dashed at the last minute. *But you should be used to disappointment,* a voice murmured treacherously in her mind. *You learned that from your adoptive parents too.*

The grey, cold weather matched her feelings as they walked back through the side streets to the car. She felt guilty. Nate had given up a precious afternoon of his free time, all for nothing. She didn't feel sorry for herself often. Right now she wished with all her heart that fairy godmothers existed, and that hers would put in a belated appearance to magic her away from the whole sorry episode.

Nate opened the door of the car for her. 'It was her loss, Jenni,' he said. She peered at him through the sleet-spattered lenses of her glasses. Inside, she felt crushed and abandoned all over again.

'Any mother would be proud to have a daughter like you.' He helped her up into the seat. The warmth of his hand on hers seared her cold flesh and he snatched his hand away, as if he had said too much.

He started the engine and pulled away from the curb. 'What are your plans for tonight?'

His question took her by surprise. She answered him before she had time to think. 'Nothing special.'

'Good,' he said. 'You can come out to dinner with me.'

She stopped wiping her glasses and turned to look at him. 'Why?'

He threaded his way through the traffic, unable to look at her as he drove. 'Why not? I'm not doing anything and neither are you. It's not been a great day, so why don't we go out and cheer ourselves up?' He made it sound so easy and reasonable.

The trouble was he seemed to be asking her for the wrong reason. She knew Nate and his 'rescuing poor Jenni' act had to stop. She'd had quite enough for one day of feeling like a charity case.

'I think I'd rather just go home. Thanks, anyway.' She schooled her voice to ensure she sounded decisive. Nate had steam-rollered her before into doing things she didn't want to do.

'If you're tired, we don't have to go out,' he countered. 'We could go to my house. Eat pizza, watch a film.' He glanced at her. 'What do you say?'

She gave a deep sigh. 'Nate, it's very kind of you, but you've done enough for me for one day. I really don't want to impose on you any longer.'

'Who said you were imposing? I thought we were friends, Jenni.' He sounded puzzled by her answer.

Jenni pondered the dilemma in silence. She didn't particularly want to go back to her grotty flat and be miserable on her own, but she didn't want people to hear she had spent personal time with her boss and get the wrong idea. She knew of Nate's devotion to Cerys' memory and felt certain he'd only asked her to dinner because he felt sorry for her. Why else would he ask her?

'Well?' They were at the traffic lights and he waited for her decision. Her brain stalled and as the lights turned green he made the move for her. 'I have to walk Rufus. We should still have time to take him out before it gets completely dark.'

Soon they were outside Nate's house. The lights were on downstairs and an old coaching lamp spilled a mellow golden glow over the front door. 'Rose, my housekeeper, leaves the lights on when she finishes for the day. Rufus is a bit of a wimp. He doesn't like the dark much.'

The wimp in question came bustling along the narrow hall to greet them both with enthusiasm at the front door. He sniffed Jenni with interest as she approached him carefully, unused to animals. *'Far too much trouble. Smelly, dirty things and what about my allergies?'* had been the response when she

42

had once dared to raise the subject at home.

Nate clipped on Rufus's lead and they set off. They took a path through an alleyway further down the street, which led to a large field. Once inside the gates, Nate took off the dog's lead. Rufus streaked away to race around and around in the dusk. His breath billowed out in white steamy bursts.

It was very dark. The cloudy sky almost eclipsed last vestiges of dull ruby sunset. A light breeze sprang up, whipping the long dead leaves from the trees at the edge of the field into little whispering heaps. Jenni shivered.

'You're cold. Come on, we'll head back.' Nate whistled. After a last interested sniff at a nearby rabbit hole, Rufus trotted obediently back.

The street lamps lit up as they made their way back to the house. As they paused on the pavement outside the gates, Jenni made a last bid to escape. 'Nate, I'm sure you'd really rather I weren't here. I can always call a cab, if you'd like.'

'Jenni, if you really want to go, I'll take you home, but if it's just some stupid pride thing of yours, then forget it.' He glared down at her. The streetlights highlighted the harsh planes of his face. 'Look, if it makes you feel better, I'd *like* you to stay. I could use some company this weekend and with you I know where I stand.' He heaved an irritated sigh and raked his hand through his hair.

'Meaning?' Nate had aroused Jenni's curiosity. He never revealed much of his inner thoughts to anyone as far as she was aware.

'You know an invitation to dinner means dinner and nothing more. Other women seem to read more into it.' He bit the words out. His dark blue gaze never left her face.

She swallowed. Well, that was plain enough. She was an asexual dinner date. Good job she didn't have an ego! 'Alright, in that case, I'd love to stay for dinner. I just didn't want you to have asked me because you felt sorry for me.' Her mouth wobbled a little as she voiced her fears. She hoped the darkness would hide the tell-tale weakness.

He grinned. 'I wouldn't dare!'

Back in the house he hung the dog lead up on the kitchen wall. 'So do you want to order in or eat out?'

'I don't mind. Whatever you prefer.' She wasn't sure about staying in with Nate. It sounded too intimate. On the other hand, she wasn't dressed up enough to frequent the kind of restaurant he probably went to.

44

'I know a good pizza place,' he suggested.

Relieved, she smiled. 'That sounds great!'

He grinned back at her as he zipped his jacket. 'And after dinner, I'll teach you how to play pool.'

She discovered he wasn't kidding. The place for pizza turned out to be next to a pool hall where Nate held a membership. After a delicious deep pan special with extra cheese, Jenni found herself in the kind of place she had been barred from for most of her life. The room was dimly lit with lots of tables all illuminated by their own yellow overhead lamps. Groups of people were at each table, they talked together in low voices as they made shots and chalked the cues.

'Come on Jen, I'll show you how to play.'

Nate demonstrated the hold and quickly potted a few shots. He showed her how to line up the ball and explained the rules.

She felt awkward as she attempted to copy how he had held the cue, and bent over the table to try a shot. He corrected her hold with a smile. His lean, deft fingers slid her hands around to place them in the right position.

Her hands shook as he removed his fingers. She bent again to take the shot. The ball ricocheted sideways and rolled to a halt in the middle of the table.

'That's not bad for a first attempt.' Nate leaned in to take his turn. The ball slid effortlessly across the baize and connected to make the pot. 'Try again, like I showed you.'

She swallowed nervously as she took her time to position her hands on the cue before trying to imitate what she had seen him do. *Oh dear heaven, he was coming to help her.* Her breath stuck at the back of her throat as he came up close behind her. He slid his arms around her to guide the position of the cue and leaned with her as she lined up the ball.

'Try to keep the action nice and smooth, don't jerk.' His breath blew warm and soft in her ear. 'Relax Jen, it isn't going to bite you.'

Her knees shook as she made the shot. To her surprise, it rolled cleanly across the table and hit the exact spot she'd been aiming for.

'There you go! Told you it was easy.'

Nate straightened up with her to watch the shot. His expression turned sober, as if he realized just how close he had been to her. She pinned a cheerful smile to her face. 'Not too bad, eh? You're a good teacher. So show me again how you held your stick thing.'

The tense moment passed and he shook

his head, laughing. 'Cue, Jenni. It's called a cue.'

The evening passed all too quickly. She soon discovered a natural aptitude for the game. Nate's praise for her blossoming skills filled her with a warm glow of pleasure. He also appeared to enjoy the evening. For once, the ever-present ghost of Cerys seemed to have left him. She wondered if the anniversary of the accident had been the real reason he hadn't wanted to be alone this weekend.

He refused to allow her to call a taxi and insisted on driving her home. The disappointment and grief of the afternoon's futile wait at the café seemed a million miles away, although her heart still felt sore at her mother's failure to show up. In many ways it had been like being left all over again. The feeling of not being good enough, which had been stamped on her from childhood, still lingered in her heart.

As the car slid to a halt, she realized they had arrived outside her flat. Now what? She had no experience of the etiquette for this sort of situation. Should she ask him in for coffee? It seemed rude not to, but Lorna had once said that coffee was a euphemism for other things. After what Nate had said earlier about other women's expectations, she didn't want to give him the wrong impression.

'Thank you for everything today, Nate.'

He smiled at her, but his eyes stayed serious and businesslike. 'It was my pleasure, Jenni. I enjoyed your company. I'm sorry your mother didn't show.'

'Well, you did warn me not to get my hopes up.' But the hurt resurfaced to settle like a stone in her stomach.

'I'd better get back to Rufus.'

Relief tinged with regret swept through her. 'Well, goodnight. See you Monday.'

He leaned across her to open the door.

'Goodnight, Jen.' His lips brushed her cheek. Her heart and pulse soared. She climbed down from the car with shaking legs and slammed the door shut. She steeled herself not to look back before she hurried across the road as if the devil himself were after her.

CHAPTER THREE

It had been a lovely evening. Jenni had been nice, funny and a good companion before he'd spoilt everything and kissed her. She'd shot out of the car like he'd grown an extra head. It had only been a peck on the cheek! A gesture of friendship, that's all.

He pulled to a halt outside his house and switched off the engine. If being with her was a mere friendship thing, why did he feel as he if he had stuck his finger in a power socket every time he touched her? This was *Jenni,* for goodness sake, his secretary.

He sighed as he let himself into the house. Rufus padded up to meet him, pushing his nose into Nate's hand in a gesture of welcome. Nate realized for the whole evening he hadn't once thought about Cerys. He wandered into the lounge, snapped on a lamp and poured himself a drink. The raw edge of the scotch on the back of his throat made his eyes water. Cerys, beautiful Cerys, his perfect woman.

Nate sank down in a leather armchair. He

swished the glass in his hand back and forth, watching the amber liquid swirl. Memories of the accident crept back into his mind. An insidious nightmare that refused to leave him. Cerys – tall, blonde and beautiful with her smiling face. He closed his eyes, but she still remained there, her green eyes bright with laughter. Then the memories of the accident came – the screech of the tires fighting for a grip on the wet road. The sound of Cerys screaming, hands grabbing at the wheel, the struggle to control the inevitable, then an almighty crash, and silence.

That had been the worse part. The silence. It had seemed to go on forever before a welcoming tide of darkness had taken him over and he had woken in a hospital bed. He opened his eyes and took another swig of whisky. A sick feeling of guilt overwhelmed him. Only yesterday he had taken flowers to her grave. He had no right to be out with another woman, even if it had only been Jenni.

He swallowed the rest of his scotch in a single gulp and turned off the lamp, then headed upstairs to bed with Rufus trotting at his heels.

Jenni watched from the window as Nate's car rolled out of sight, before letting the curtain drop back into place. Her cheek burned as if she had been branded and her skin still tingled from where his lips had touched her. Anyone would think she'd never been kissed before. Well, not many times before, but those had been on the lips, and hadn't made her feel so...

Jenni paused in her self-analysis, not sure she wanted to go there. It had been a long day. She had been over-emotional. Nate had taken pity on her. He must kiss lots of women in the same way. It was just a sociable gesture. She ignored the niggling ache in her heart which betrayed her true feelings.

After she changed for bed, she replaced her precious photograph back in her keepsake box. Jenni wondered if she would ever hear from her mother again.

She woke the next day with a mild headache and a discontented, out-of-sorts feeling. She thought back to the previous night and searched for what had triggered the restless, dissatisfied mood which had her in its grip. Irritated with herself, she flung open the wardrobe doors and gazed at her clothes.

'You know an invitation to dinner means just that.' Nate's words haunted her. In other words, she wasn't the kind of woman men saw as a desirable dinner date. And he could

have a point. She wasn't over-run with offers, was she?

Maybe she should take Lorna's advice and revamp herself. Enter the dating game. It wasn't as if she was ugly, just dowdy. Jenni didn't have much cash, but she did have a sewing machine and she knew how to use it. Before she could change her mind, she started to pull the hangers from her closet. She tugged out her sewing machine from the bottom of the cupboard.

Later that night, Jenni surveyed her day's handiwork with a satisfied smile. A few alterations on seams and hems had made quite a difference, but she would need some advice from Lorna about her hair and make-up. Lorna always looked smart, and she bought all the latest fashion magazines. Her friend would be bound to have some good ideas.

Jenni felt self-conscious of her appearance as she walked through the revolving doors of the office building the next morning. The seams she had altered showed her slim waist to advantage and the shorter hem revealed long, shapely legs. It was a respectable and appropriate outfit for work, but in the glass atrium of reality, she felt over-exposed.

Lorna waved to her from the reception

desk and Jenni hurried over.

'You look different,' Lorna announced. 'I don't know what you've done, but you look great.'

'I'll tell you everything at lunchtime.' Jenni automatically smoothed her skirt.

Lorna lifted an immaculately pencilled eyebrow. 'Sounds interesting! What have you been up to over the weekend?'

Jenni caught sight of the time and cut her friend short. 'I promise I'll tell you later. I've got to go. It's the monthly meeting and I daren't be late.'

She squeezed in to the lift as the door started to close. The other occupant was a member of the accountancy team, a young man who appeared to blush as much as she did.

'It's Jenni, isn't it? Mr Mayer's P.A? I'm Mike, I work in accounts.' He stammered a little as he spoke. Jenni couldn't help feeling a bit sorry for him. She knew what it felt like to be shy.

'Yes, I'm Jenni. I thought I saw you at the meeting last month.'

The lift door opened and he followed her out onto the landing. 'I, erm, just wanted to say you look very nice today,' he called after her.

Jenni knew she must be as scarlet as a poppy. She paused, feeling awkward, her hand on the office door handle. She called back, 'Thank you.'

The door opened in front of her before she had time to turn the handle, taking her by surprise. She cannoned into Nate's chest and bumped her nose against his chin.

'When you've finished flirting, Jenni, we've got a meeting.'

Her breath whooshed out of her at his sudden appearance. Shaken, she stared up at him. All the small pleasure of Mike's compliment evaporated along with most of her good mood.

'I'll just be a minute,' she heard herself say as she slipped past him into the office.

The door slammed shut behind her and she heard the deep rumble of Nate's voice through the wall as he greeted the other staff in the boardroom.

The meeting passed by in a blur. The workload was fast and furious as they had a prestigious job to tender for in New York. Their American agent had done as much as she was able to, so now it depended on the reception their designs and prices received.

'You'll need to check your passport is valid

if this project goes through, Jenni,' Nate said as she tidied up the post meeting debris.

She almost dropped her stack of cups. 'I don't have a passport.' She blurted the words out before she even thought to ask him why she needed one. Nate had such an expression of incredulity on his face she almost laughed out loud.

'No passport? You mean you've never left the country or that it's expired?'

She carried on placing the dirty cups on the tray. 'I've never had a passport. I've never been abroad, unless you count the Isle of Wight when I was three.'

He stood staring at her in disbelief. She returned his gaze with a hint of a challenge, daring him to make something of it.

'Well, you'd better get one sorted out quickly. If this all goes ahead, which I feel sure it will, you'll be coming to New York with me in January.'

She wasn't sure what to say. The prospect of traveling excited her, but to go so far away, and with Nate. A mixture of emotions whizzed through her brain with irritation surfaced that he took it for granted that she would come.

'A little notice would have been nice,' she suggested.

He frowned. 'This isn't something new, Jenni. I know I haven't asked you to travel before, but we did discuss the possibility when you took the job. Are you telling me you don't want to go?'

She paused with the tray in her hands. 'No. It's just that, well, I might have had plans.'

A trace of a smile tugged at the corner of his mouth. *Just let him laugh,* she thought, as she banged the sugar bowl down.

'And did you?' he asked, his voice smooth. 'Have plans?'

She could see amusement glinting in his eyes. She gathered up the tray and her self-esteem with as much dignity as she could muster. 'As it happens, I haven't anything definite.'

She swept into the tiny kitchen where the conference supplies were kept and whacked the tray down hard on the counter. She threw the cups into the sink, then scrubbed them with a ferocity they didn't deserve before going downstairs to meet Lorna for lunch.

She filled her friend in on her weekend over a cheese salad sandwich in the café down the road. For the first time in ages, she didn't feel guilty at the expense and splurged on chocolate muffins for dessert. Lorna rewarded her with undivided attention as Jenni told her about her mother and her evening with Nate. The kiss part she kept to herself.

'I've been telling you for ages to make more of yourself, Jen. I didn't know you were so good on the sewing machine though. A night out with the boss too, things are looking up!' Mischief danced in Lorna's eyes as she smiled at Jenni.

Jenni sighed and sipped her tea, ignoring Lorna's teasing. 'You don't think I'm making a fool of myself, then?'

Lorna stared at her. 'Why would you be making a fool of yourself? You're entitled to a life, Jenni. You're young with a fantastic figure, a pretty face and a great personality.' She grinned and licked a piece of chocolate from her finger. 'Mike from Accounts really likes you.'

Jenni shook her head in reproof at Loma's blatant hint. 'Yeah right! Like he'd be interested in me! Come on, look at the time. I daren't be late twice in one day.

Nate watched Jenni depart in a huff along the corridor. He wasn't quite sure what was different about her today. She looked the same. Well, almost the same. But he didn't remember noticing she had such great legs before, or the way her skirt fitted so very nicely over her hips.

No wonder Mike Walker had started to pay her attention. Jenni deserved better than some wet-behind-the-ears moneyman, but she had shot off to lunch pretty quickly and Nate couldn't help but wonder who she had been lunching with.

He heard Jenni sneak back into the office after her lunch break. The tell-tale squeak of her chair as she slid it out from under the desk gave her away. He looked at his watch, realizing she had taken the full hour and had just about made it back in time. Jenni never took her full break. Maybe she *had* been to meet Mike. For some reason, the thought didn't please Nate at all.

'Did you have a nice lunch?'

Jenni gave a guilty start as Nate entered the office. Had he noticed she'd been a few minutes late?

'Lovely, thanks.' Nate in a bad mood could be very trying. She wished he would go back to his own office. She hated it when he kept hanging around. It made it so hard to concentrate on her work.

'Go anywhere nice?' He drummed a pen

58

against the top of her desk.

Her temper rose. What on earth was the matter with him today?

'Only to the café down the road. Did you forget something, Nate? I need to get on.' She kept her fingers poised over the keyboard and willed him to go away.

'I just wanted to let you know that we have a hectic time ahead of us. I'm afraid it will mean a lot of late nights and some weekend work.'

She looked at him and tried to interpret the expression on his face. He didn't often bother telling her they needed to do extra hours. 'That's okay, I could use the money,' she said.

'What I mean, Jenni, is it might not be a good time to, you know, get involved with anyone.' He stopped the irritating drumming to lean casually against the desk.

Now he really had her beat. She was horrified. Was he hinting that she shouldn't get ideas about *him?* Of all the conceited...!

'I wasn't aware my private life was any concern of yours, and if you think for one moment I would be interested in you, then you can think again.'

He drew himself up to his full height. She knew by the frosty look on his face she had said something out of turn.

'I was referring to your friend Mr Walker,' he announced in a glacial tone. Before she had time to respond, his door slammed shut and he was gone.

'Well, that told you,' she muttered.

How to completely humiliate yourself in one easy lesson. It was just as well she'd never thought of Nate in a romantic light. Well, except for one very nice dream she'd had the other night.

She switched off that particular memory.

Nate's door exploded open. 'Have you done those memos yet?'

'Almost,' she lied, and started to type, forcing herself to concentrate on her work.

The morning turned into a long and horrible afternoon. By the time she'd finished her work, the cleaners had started to vacuum the carpet in the corridor outside her office. Her head pounded with the noise.

She switched off her monitor with a sigh. Nate still remained in his office, hard at work. Darkness had fallen outside, and as she turned off her desk lamp, she realized she felt both tired and hungry. She rapped on Nate's door, then pushed it open and carried on in. 'Nate, I'm going home now.

Are you done yet?'

He looked as tired as she felt. Dark circles had formed under his eyes. Stubble showed in a faint shadow along the line of his jaw.

'I'll take you home. I've had enough for today.' He switched off his computer and stood up to pull his jacket from the back of his chair.

Even with her higher heeled shoes he still loomed over her, a fact she had half registered earlier in the day when she had cannoned into him in the doorway. He locked the design cabinet, then switched off his office light.

She trailed along the corridor behind him to the lift. The doors chimed open as they reached the deserted lobby. The onyx reception desk stood empty. Lorna had gone home much earlier. Only the uniformed security guard remained in the building to make his routine nighttime patrol.

'I can catch the bus, Nate. It would save you from going out of your way.'

He checked the messages in the 'in' tray. 'No, I'll take you. It's dark and freezing out there.' He paused in his paper shuffling. 'There's something here for you, Jen.'

She accepted the slip of paper from him and started to read before she registered why the rounded, childlike scrawl appeared familiar.

Her mother's words leapt up at her from the cheap lined paper.

'Sorry I couldn't get away to meet you. I'll be in touch when things are better.'

The signature said Tracey, her birth mother's first name. The letters swam in front of Jenni's eyes. Her knees had all the strength of marshmallows. A strong arm encircled her waist as Nate steered her into Lorna's chair.

The guard's footsteps rang muzzily in her ears. She heard him confer in an urgent tone with Nate. The buzzing noises receded as she came back to reality. Nate squatted on his haunches at her feet.

'I'm sorry. I don't know what happened.' She never fainted. What's been happening to her lately?

'I thought you were going to pass right out. You looked as white as a ghost.' He looked concerned.

'I'm fine, honestly.'

His nearness made her nervous. The faint masculine scent of his cologne tugged at her senses. She stood up, her knees still weak. 'It seems to be my day for making a fool of myself.'

'I'll drive you home.' He placed his arm around her waist once more, causing her to give an instinctive jerk at the intimacy of the gesture.

Nate's heart raced as he supported Jenni on the walk across the car park. He could feel the soft, yielding warmth of her body as he steadied her. It had been a long time since he had held a woman so closely. Too long. Jenni's femininity and her closeness stirred deep-seated emotions he had never expected to feel again.

He relinquished his support with relief when they reached the car. Her proximity disturbed him in ways he didn't want to admit. She accepted his help to climb in with a murmur of thanks.

'How do you feel now?'

She looked at him. 'I'm okay, just feeling rather foolish. I've never fainted before in my life.'

'It was a bit of a shock. I asked the security guard if he knew who'd left the note, but he hadn't seen anyone.'

She seemed to be digesting the information. 'If Lorna had been there, she would have contacted me straight away, so it must have been after she finished work.'

He grunted an assent. It sounded logical.

Jenni must have spoken to Lorna about the weekend's events. He wondered how much she had told her, not that anything needed to be hidden.

There had been enough rumors after the accident, along with numerous well-meaning women who had all appeared to be convinced he needed a shoulder on which to cry. Well, he hadn't. Nate didn't subscribe to the idea that talking about things made them any better. He'd discharged himself from the hospital as soon as possible after the accident and had refused to see the bereavement counselor.

He glanced across at Jenni. Behind those awful glasses she wore, her tired eyes looked sad. He hated the thought of dropping her off at her tiny flat and leaving her on her own.

He pulled the car to a halt in the lay-by opposite her home. The takeaway appeared to be doing good business amongst the teenagers.

'Thank you for the lift.' She paused as if trying to come to a decision. 'You're welcome to come in and have some supper with me, if you like.'

Her suggestion took him by surprise. He'd

had the feeling the other day that she hadn't been comfortable with inviting him in. She had appeared awkward and diffident, very different from the young woman he thought he knew.

Second thoughts occurred to Jenni even before she opened the front door and snapped on the light. Nate sank into her armchair, weariness stamped all over his frame. A little pain pierced her heart as she looked at him. She clamped down hard on the feeling. Nate was her friend and her boss. Nothing more.

She escaped into the kitchen to prepare the supper before she could betray herself. Nate switched on the television and she heard the noise of some motoring program.

Her cupboards were pretty empty as she hadn't had chance to go shopping for a few days. She examined the contents of her fridge and popped her head around the door to ask if he liked omelettes, only to find he'd dozed off.

He appeared so vulnerable, sprawled in her tatty throw-covered armchair. His long legs stretched out in front of him and the stubble on his chin showed dark against the faint olive of his skin. She stood for a moment, just watching, and then feeling as if she had done something illicit, turned back to her cooking.

Fifteen minutes later, she had two fluffy ham and cheese omelettes and salad ready on trays. She wished she'd had something more original to offer him, but at least the food smelt good. Nate remained asleep in the armchair. She wondered how to wake him.

'Nate.'

He didn't stir, so she placed a tentative hand on his arm and shook him. 'Supper's ready.'

He groaned and pulled himself straight while he rubbed his eyes. 'Sorry, Jenni. I'm not very good company tonight.' She passed him a tray. He sniffed the food with appreciation. 'Smells great.'

Nate ate his dinner like a starving man. Soon both their plates were empty. It felt nice to have company in her flat. Most evenings she was there on her own. He refused another cup of tea, and sounded reluctant as he pulled on his jacket before announcing he had to go.

Jenni followed him down the narrow stairs so she could slip the chain across on the door after he'd gone. He stepped outside onto the pavement.

'Don't stay down here, Jenni. It's too cold.' His dark blue eyes locked with hers. She tried to read his thoughts. Without any warning, his head dipped and his lips brushed against hers in a sweet but all-too-brief caress before he went leaving her cold and alone in the hallway.

CHAPTER FOUR

Jenni watched Nate leave before she closed her door and trudged back up the dingy stairs to her flat. What a day! One minute Nate had been as grouchy as a bear with a sore head and the next moment he kissed her.

The downside soon followed the high of his kiss. Nate was still her boss. He didn't see her in any kind of romantic light. He still grieved for the beautiful fiancé he had lost under such awful circumstances two years earlier. To fall for Nate would be a bad idea. A *very* bad idea.

She peeled off her clothes and promised herself a few days away from work as soon as things quietened down in the office. She hadn't taken any holiday for months. It would be nice to have the time to do some more painting. Art restored her spirits and a little restoration sounded good about now.

She clicked off the bedside light after she hopped into bed. Christmas presented a whole other bundle of problems. Like what to do with herself whilst everyone else spent time with their loved ones. Last year, she'd spent the festive season alone in her flat with the television for company and a frozen chicken dinner for one. She closed her eyes and snuggled down under the duvet with a hollow feeling in her heart.

The following week passed by in a blur of late hours. Nate retreated back into boss mode. Apart from the nights when he insisted on giving her a lift home, they never seemed to be alone together.

When her phone rang on Friday afternoon, Jenni had the start of a tension headache.

'Are you all set for tomorrow then?' Lorna chirped.

She had finally relented to Lorna's nagging about going shopping for new clothes and make-up, but Jenni already had second thoughts about it. She hadn't spent much money on herself for what seemed like forever.

'If I must,' she said, only half joking. The idea of change excited her, but Lorna's enthusiasm for the project was overwhelming.

'Don't tell me you're feeling chicken? Listen, pop down later and see me if you get a chance. I'll show you what I've arranged.

It's going to be great.'

Jenni hung up to cross the office, ready to feed the invitations for the Christmas dance into the photocopier. She stood and waited for it to churn out the copies. She had never been to the dance before. The first year she had worked for Nate, her mother had been too ill for Jenni to feel comfortable about leaving her. Last year, it had been too soon after her death. Jenni hadn't felt like celebrating.

Nate had already made it clear he expected her to go this year. She had done all the planning for it, organized the decorations, the band and even the presents. Maybe she should use the opportunity to show off a new look.

The light on the copier started to blink and Jenni ducked down to reload the paper tray. She straightened back up to restart the copies, only to find herself face-to-face with Mike Walker. He picked up one of the party invitations. 'Christmas dance?' he read out loud from the leaflet, oblivious to Jenni's burning cheeks.

'Yes, it's at the Langstone Club this year.' She scooped up the copies. A strong, sickly aroma of cheap aftershave assailed her nostrils as he moved a little closer to her.

'It's that new hotel-cum-country club on the outskirts. It's supposed to be very exclusive.' Jenni explained.

Mike handed her back the leaflet. She noticed his round, pleasant face looked rather flushed. 'I wonder if you would like to, erm, that is... I ... if you wanted to go with me to the dance?'

'I'm afraid that won't be possible.' Nate's voice cut in.

Mike turned even redder. Beads of perspiration appeared under the fringe of his fair hair.

'Jenni is accompanying me and acting as my hostess for the evening, so I'm afraid she'll be rather busy.' Nate's diamond gaze and confident tone quelled any possible argument.

Jenni watched impotently as her would-be suitor muttered an apologetic excuse and bolted down the corridor back to the safety of the accounts department.

'How dare you! That was a private conversation!' She wanted to strangle him, as he stood there looking smug whilst her first chance of a date in over a year evaporated in front of her eyes.

'Jenni, I did warn you that we were too busy right now for you to be expanding your social life.' He appeared unperturbed.

'It would have been nice if you had told me beforehand that you expected me to act as hostess. Or even, Heaven forbid, you might have considered actually asking me. The way you came crashing in just then, Mike might get quite the wrong idea about us. I mean, me.'

He stared at her in amazement. 'Jenni, I don't think that's going to happen, do you? You're my P.A. You know everyone in the company and you've organized the whole event. Who better to hostess it with me?' On that reasonable-sounding note he disappeared back into his office.

Once inside the safety of his office, Nate wondered what had possessed him to intervene when Mike Walker had asked Jenni out. It was none of his business. Jenni had a right to be angry.

Walker wouldn't get the wrong idea about Nate's relationship with Jenni. Would he? Unless Jenni herself had ideas about their friendship... He rubbed his chin as he paced up and down in front of the desk deep in thought.

Surely she wouldn't, she had always seemed much too sensible. He'd never thought of Jenni as a frivolous kind of girl. She never fussed about her appearance the way some women did. Like Cerys had. Cerys' voice rang in his memory,

'Appearances count, darling. I know you laugh but if you want to get anywhere in life then you must dress for success.'

He paused in his pacing. Cerys *had* dressed for success. Her clothes had all been designer labels, her nails had always been manicured and her hairdresser had been on permanent standby. She had masked her insecurities with an armor of perfection so refined he hadn't noticed the price she had been prepared to pay until it was too late.

He bit down hard on that train of thought. Jenni was not Cerys. No, Jenni knew where she stood, didn't she? A momentary feeling of disquiet flitted through his mind. Jenni had started to change her appearance in the last couple of weeks. Higher heels, more fitted clothes. No wonder Walker kept hanging about her like a lovesick puppy. Jenni was a very attractive girl. The kind of girl he could be attracted to.

He scowled at the view from his window and wished the young accounts manager a million miles away from Mayer holdings and Jenni Blake.

'It looks great, Jen. Really it does.' Lorna assured her.

Jenni squinted at her hair in the mirror. Nate's colossal insensitivity had made her brave. He'd made it very clear that he didn't find her at all attractive. That there was no way anyone would think he could ever be interested in her romantically. Well, come Monday morning, Nathanial Mayer would see another side to Jenni Blake.

It had been Lorna's idea to go to the beauty college open day. So far they had both had manicures, massages and pedicures – all for a token sum of money. Now she had a new hairstyle and autumn tints in her hair.

Lorna pulled the plastic cape from Jenni's shoulders 'Anyway, come on. We've got a facial and make-up demo next. After lunch, we're going shopping. The first stop is at the opticians.'

Jenni wished her bravado hadn't led her quite this far. Her naturally cautious nature rebelled a little at the idea of spending so much time and money on herself, even if it was fun. She thanked the hairdresser and followed Lorna into the next department.

By the end of a very long day it came as a

blissful relief to open the door of her flat and stagger inside. Her arms ached with the weight of the bags she carried. Her new contact lenses made her blink like an owl.

She hung up her new clothes and kicked off her shoes. A long, hot bath called to her to soak her weary limbs. Armed with a glass of the cheap white wine she kept in the fridge, she lay amongst the bubbles and tried to ignore the cracked tile on the opposite wall. At long last, aching muscles relaxed. She hadn't realized looking beautiful was so high maintenance.

She lazed among the suds until the water cooled. After toweling herself dry she pulled on her old fleecy grey dressing gown, tied the cord around her narrow waist and headed into the kitchen to fix herself a sandwich.

The doorbell rang as she buttered the bread. Quite often the gang of teenagers who loitered outside the takeaway amused themselves by ringing her bell. This caused her to hesitate as she wondered if she should ignore it or take a peek to see if she really had a caller.

The doorbell sounded again. Jenni put the knife down and walked across the lounge to lift the curtain to peep out through the window. A familiar figure in a black leather jacket stood in the rain outside her front door. Astonished, she almost let the curtain drop back into place when Nate looked up and noticed her.

Flustered, Jenni looked at her ratty old dressing gown. There wasn't time to change. He would be soaked if he stayed out there in the wet for much longer. She hurried down the stairs to let him in, grateful the thick material covered her body so well.

When Jenni opened the front door, Nate stepped inside so quickly she found herself trapped at the foot of the stairs with him. In the tiny confines of the dark hallway, she could almost feel the warmth of his breath on her cheek.

'Nate. I wasn't expecting company.' Her voice squeaked. Nate stood too close to her for comfort, much too close.

'Come up to the flat.' Jenni fought the panic rising in her chest, and half-turned to escape up the stairs, desperate to put some space between them.

Nate remained still, staring at her, a bewildered expression on his face. 'Where are your glasses?' The rainwater dripped off the hem of his coat and made a puddle on the floor.

'You're wet.' Jenni licked her lips nervously.

'And your hair. You've had your hair cut.'

He touched one of the chopped-off strands of her hair with tentative fingers. She couldn't tell if he approved of the changes or not. *Not that it's got anything to do with him,* she thought.

'It's not against the law, is it?'

Her sharp response snapped him out of his trance-like state.

'I was just surprised, that's all.' He shrugged.

Not entirely satisfied with his answer, she led the way up the stairs, into the flat. It wouldn't kill him to say he liked her improved appearance, would it?

'You'd better give me your coat and I'll hang it over the bath tub to dry.'

He unzipped his jacket, conscious he still stared at her.

She reached over to take his coat. He smelt the fresh, soapy scent of her skin.

'This was a bad idea of mine to call without phoning you first, Jenni. I'm obviously in your way.'

Had she got anything on underneath that hideous dressing gown? The palms of his hands were wet with sweat, and it came as a relief when she vanished into the bathroom with his jacket.

Jenni reappeared. 'Sit down, Nate. I'll get you a drink.'

He sat down on the edge of Jenni's settee, taking care to avoid the broken spring. She disappeared into the kitchen. It was like trying to talk to a human yo-yo.

'I came to ask you a favor.' He wished she would come back in and sit down.

'Coffee all right?' Jenni's disembodied voice asked from the kitchen.

'Fine.'

She re-emerged, carrying a tray with two mugs and a couple of plates with sandwiches. 'I thought you might be hungry, I was just about to eat,' she explained. 'You were saying you wanted to ask me a favor?' She passed him a plate. The top of her dressing gown gaped open a little before she moved back to perch on the old armchair by the gas fire.

Either the heating in her flat was up too high, or the brief flash of Jenni's bare skin had made him feel quite hot. She looked so different without her glasses, and she did have beautiful eyes. Deep ... sparkling ... blue...

He realized he hadn't answered her question. 'I came to ask if you could come into work early on Monday. A delegation is coming over from New York to meet us and discuss the project. They're flying in early, so we'll need to organize meals, accommodation and travel for them. They plan to stay one night, then they're going to London to see the opposition bid.'

She leaned forward to pick up her mug. He thought his heart would stop.

'That's okay. I know how important the bid is. I'll be there.'

He picked up his coffee and sipped it. Jenni had been right. He *was* hungry. His mother hadn't sounded too pleased when he had phoned to cancel his lunch date with his parents, pleading pressure of work.

'You'll have to let me know all the details. How many to expect, diets, flight times and so on.' A small frown puckered the creamy smooth skin of her forehead.

Even her face looked different. More sophisticated. With professionally applied make-up, she had acquired an air of glamour alien to the Jenni he knew. *He had to stop staring.*

'That's no problem. I can drop a file over to you tomorrow.' He set his mug down and started on his sandwiches. 'Thanks for these. I didn't have time to eat lunch today.'

80

She looked disapproving. 'You should make time, Nate. This was supposed to be your weekend off.'

As Jenni grabbed a sandwich, her long furry gown slipped open to reveal a great deal of her legs before she swished it back into place. He choked on a crumb. Jeep, he would have to go home. He didn't think his libido could stand many more tantalizing glimpses of Jenni's bare skin without him wanting to do something they both might regret.

'I have to go.' He placed his empty plate on the table and stood up abruptly.

She looked up at him. He could see her bewilderment at the sudden change in his behavior.

'I'll fetch your coat.' Jenni left to collect his jacket from the bathroom. 'It's dried out pretty well, so you should be okay.' She handed it to him.

'I'll drop that stuff off for you tomorrow then, if that's alright?' He slipped into his jacket. The sensible voice inside his brain told him to get the hell out of there now, before he did something stupid. The problem was his body didn't appear to be connected to his brain. All he could see were Jenni's moist, pink lips parted as if anticipating his kiss.

Even then, he might have resisted if it hadn't been for her startled little gasp when she read his intentions in his eyes.

She tasted the way he thought she would, as sweet as honey. His arms slipped around her slim waist to hold her closer. The soft, slight curves of her body molded against him, as if she had been meant to fit.

The tinny little tune from his inner jacket pocket wasn't loud enough to disturb his concentration. It took Jenni's startled response to the vibrator setting on his phone to break them apart.

He grabbed the phone from his pocket. His twin sister's phone number flashed up on the display.

Jenni stood before him, her blue eyes wide with mute distress. He felt a complete heel as he pressed the talk button on the phone and brought it to his ear.

CHAPTER FIVE

Jenni folded her arms tight across her chest and hugged herself. Dazed, she stumbled into the bathroom to splash some cool water onto her face, hoping it would wash away the delicious taste of Nate from her lips. He'd rushed off after answering his phone as if he couldn't stand to be near her a moment longer. So much for her makeover. It was supposed to make her more attractive, not more repellent.

She washed the rest of the make-up from her face, forgetting all about the morning's lecture on skin care. Her eyes stung from the new contact lenses, so she removed them in favor of her glasses. All that done, she took a deep breath.

Her adoptive father's voice sounded immediately in her mind, sending her back into her teenage years.

'I won't have you looking like a streetwalker whilst you're living under my roof, Jennifer.'

She had come home from school to discover her father had discovered her innocent little cache of make-up. She had been forced to watch him throw each piece onto the coal fire one by one while he lectured her on wanton women.

Well, she had lived down to her father's expectations tonight. Nate hadn't exactly beaten her off, but the horrified look on his face when the phone had interrupted them would stay with her for a long time.

'Nicely brought up girls do not behave like that, Jennifer. There were so many rules and regulations on what might be considered proper and decent. What *nice* girls did and didn't do. Somehow, no matter how hard she had tried to please them, she had always managed to disappoint.

A lump came into her throat and she swallowed hard. She blinked back the tears which threatened to creep from under her closed eyelids as she remembered the day she had first realized that no matter how hard she tried, her parents were never going to be proud of her.

She had run home from school that day, eager to tell her mother her exciting news. She had been chosen from the whole school for her artistic ability and had won a special prize for her drawing. Her photograph would be in the local paper and she would receive a case full of artist's materials at an official presentation.

She'd hurtled in through the back door on that hot and sunny afternoon, impatient to share her joy. The story had come tumbling from her lips as she had panted breathlessly in the kitchen, dizzy from having run all the way home. Her mother listened in stony-faced silence while Jenni had explained about the competition.

'I don't recall your father or me giving permission for you to participate in this kind of non-academic frivolity.' Jenni stared at her mother's disapproving face and, at eight years old, had learned the things that she was good at – art, music and dance – had no value in her parents' world. There had been no presentation, no art case and no photograph. Another child, the little boy who had come second, had been declared the winner. Her father caused a scene at the school and there had been no more competition entries for Jenni.

Except her parents hadn't won. She had continued to paint. Her artwork was an important part of her life. One day she planned to organize a showing of her work. The thought of her paintings only served to remind her of Nate again. What should she do? She couldn't avoid him. He was due to come over tomorrow to give her the file so she could help him prepare for the delegation's arrival on Monday.

Somehow, she would have to convince Nate that kissing him had been a one-off event. It meant nothing to her and would never be repeated. Her pride wouldn't allow him to think she'd enjoyed it. Especially as his reaction had showed how clearly he'd regretted kissing her.

The problem was, she thought as she tidied up before switching off the lights and going to bed, she wouldn't mind repeating the experience. Kissing Nate felt like a habit she could quite happily become addicted to.

Nate was on the receiving end of a telephone lecture from his sister.

'There is more to life than work, Nate. Mum's really upset with you for cancelling at the last minute. And it's not as though this is the first time either. Much as we love you, you're pushing it. You really are. It's been two years now since … well. You can't duck out of life forever.' Her voice softened and he tried to interrupt.

'It's my life, Nathalie. I've a big contract lined up, the biggest we've ever had. I need to have everything in place for Monday.'

His twin gave a snort of dismissal. 'Your company is big enough, Nate. You've already proved everything you ever wanted to. You've lived and breathed nothing else since the accident. How many millions will it take to make you happy, Nate? It won't solve the real problem.'

No one else except Nathalie ever dared to talk to him like this. Even she had tiptoed around him for the last two years, frightened of saying the wrong thing.

'What was wrong when I called you tonight?' she demanded. 'You sounded like you wanted to kill me.'

Nate sighed. 'It just wasn't great timing, that's all.'

'Why?' she asked. 'Where were you? You weren't at home, I tried that number first.'

'I was at Jenni's,' he snapped, and wished he could take the words back.

'Jenni? Your P.A.? You didn't make that poor girl work on a Saturday night, did you?' Nathalie sounded scandalized. 'I honestly don't know why she works for you. I really don't. It's not as if you appreciate all the things she does for you.'

In contrast, Nate thought he would have liked nothing better than to have spent more time appreciating Jenni.

'Are you listening to me?' Nathalie must have continued talking during his trance.

'It wasn't work. Well, not entirely... I...' He groaned and decided to stop digging. His words had already made him a big enough hole. But Nathalie had been quick to pick up on his remark and the tone of her voice changed.

'Oh...' Her voice sounded heavy with meaning. 'I see, maybe you are starting to move on. In that case, I'm sorry. I did call at a bad time.' Her low husky chuckle rang in his ear. 'You should have said something before and I would have spared you the lecture. Well, apologize to Jenni for me, won't you. She's such a nice girl, I like her. I'll call you in the week.'

Jenni didn't sleep well. She stood in front of her bathroom mirror the next morning and toyed with the idea of leaving her new lenses in their case. But if the visiting delegation were due to arrive the next day, then she owed it to Nate to look groomed and stylish. Even if he didn't approve of her new look.

She scurried around the flat as she caught up on a week's worth of neglected chores. A quick inventory of the contents of her fridge told her she needed to go out for groceries.

There wasn't even enough milk for her morning coffee.

She shrugged on the new coat that Lorna had convinced her was a bargain and grabbed her bag, ready to walk the few streets to the all day supermarket. If Nate came while she was out, he could push the file through her letterbox. Her heart fell into her shoes at the idea. It would be embarrassing seeing Nate again after last night, but the possibility that she might miss him felt even worse.

When she rounded the corner an hour later, laden down with bags, Nate's tall muscular figure crossed the road towards her.

'Let me help you.'

Before she could protest, he had taken most of the carriers from her grasp and set off with long strides towards her front door. She fumbled in her pocket for her door key with her free hand.

'I wasn't expecting you yet.'

Nate stood aside to let her open the door. He followed as she led the way up the stairs. She opened the flat door and headed for the kitchen to deposit the heavy bags.

'Where do you want the carriers put?' He was right behind her. His proximity both excited and disturbed her in the small space.

'Just drop them down there and have a

seat. I'll put the kettle on.' Time spent stowing away the shopping would provide a welcome respite from his closeness. To her annoyance he lingered in the kitchen.

He watched while she opened and closed cupboards and drawers, knocking over and spilling the contents in her haste to tidy everything away.

'After yesterday I didn't know whether to call first, or just to come around,' Nate said.

'Have you brought the file with you?' Jenni fumbled in the cutlery drawer for a spoon, determined to keep the conversation on a professional level. Okay, so she was attracted to him. It was fine, everything was cool. She could deal with this.

He reached in the inside pocket of his jacket for a long fat envelope which he placed on the counter. 'All present and correct. I'll run through it with you so you'll know where things stand.'

'We'll go in the lounge and you can brief me on everything.'

Jenni sat in the seat furthest away from his. Her blue eyes wide as she sipped her drink, the ruffled edges of her hair made her look as if she had just tumbled out of bed.

The unexpected thought caused Nate to

slop a little of the hot coffee over the edge of his mug onto his thumb. He put the drink down quickly and sucked the burning fluid off his hand. What was the matter with him?

He opened the envelope he had brought with him to begin briefing her on who she should expect in the delegation.

Jenni made cryptic little squiggles on a notepad. After she read back over her notes, she made a few suggestions about the plans he'd outlined. She rested her pencil against the corner of her mouth when she paused.

Nate's attention strayed to where the pencil eraser pressed against the soft pink skin of her lips. Lips which had aroused feelings he had thought he could no longer feel.

'Nate?' Jenni frowned at him. She must have asked him some question he simply hadn't heard.

'Sorry Jen, I didn't hear you. I was thinking.' Good job she didn't know *what* he'd been thinking, or he suspected he would have been thrown out of her flat with the same speed that he had been told to leave the previous night.

'I see.' She frowned again and placed her pad down on the coffee table. 'Nate, about what happened last night...' Her eyes were troubled. A chill of foreboding ran through him. *Please don't let her resign.*

'Jenni...'

She held her hand up to stop him from speaking. 'I think we should forget about what happened between us last night. It was a mistake and won't ever happen again.'

'It won't?' He should feel reassured by her statement, relieved that she didn't appear to want to change the basis of their friendship. Instead, depression settled over his head like a rain cloud that refused to go away.

She flushed and her eyes met his. 'It won't,' she confirmed. She tucked her hair back behind her ears and surveyed him levelly. Her words hit him with the same physical impact as a thump in the stomach. Nate struggled to find the right words to express how he felt.

'You're right, Jenni. I shouldn't have taken advantage of the situation. I'm sorry.' He had to focus, remember Jenni was his secretary. He should be pleased with her decision.

'Then the sooner we both forget about it the better, we need to go back to a normal working relationship.' Her eyes looked a little over-bright when she made her statement, but she sounded determined.

'In that case, I'm taking you out for Sunday lunch. I owe you for all the extra work you've done this morning and a civilized lunch would help restore things to the proper perspective.' He told himself he should be pleased that Jenni didn't want to get involved with him romantically. His life would become simpler. Things would go back to normal.

She looked doubtful, as if she wasn't sure about his motives. In fairness, he couldn't blame her.

'We are still friends, I hope, Jenni.' He prayed she wouldn't refuse. It was important to him that he got their old easygoing friendship back. Then everything would settle down again and he could carry on as he had before. A bleak sense of loneliness filled his soul as he snuffed out the tiny flame of hope that flared for a short time in his heart.

Jenni felt a little deflated as she clambered into Nate's car and buckled her seatbelt. She'd got what she wanted, hadn't she?

More to the point, why had she agreed to go out to lunch with Nate? When she had opened her mouth she had planned to politely and tactfully decline his offer.

She had to get a grip. Nate still loved Cerys. He had made it quite clear in the past how he viewed Jenni, as a mate, not a date. He had jumped at her plan to return

93

to normal working partnership.

'Everywhere will be busy. Where are we going?' She wondered if they would be able to find anywhere with a free table at the last minute.

'I thought we'd go to the Langstone. Test-drive the restaurant before the party next week.' He glanced at her. Jenni raised her chin, remembering the disagreement of Friday when he had scuppered her date for the party.

'Sounds good. But I thought you'd been there before?'

'I joined just after it opened. It was Nathalie's idea. She goes there quite often. She recommended it when I was after a venue for the staff party. I've only been a few times myself.'

They turned off the main road onto a long, tree-lined private driveway. Jenni recalled the glossy brochure she had received on booking the party. The large stone portico led into a marble-floored entrance hall, where a glittery crystal chandelier twinkled overhead.

The restaurant was huge. On one side of the room floor-to-ceiling picture windows afforded a panoramic view of the Japanese water gardens and gazebos. Dark oak paneling divided part of the room into smaller booths for more private dining. The waiter showed them to a quiet table with a view of the gardens.

As the man pulled out her chair, Jenni noticed the huge array of cutlery on the snowy tablecloth in front of her. A ball of panic rose in her stomach.

'I wasn't expecting it to be this,' she struggled to find the right words. 'Glamorous.'

'This is the member's restaurant. The staff party will be in one of the function rooms. I believe this place is popular for weddings now.' He smiled at her. 'We could always go back to the pizza restaurant if you prefer.'

She smiled back at him. 'No, this is fine. It was just a surprise, that's all.'

The waiter returned with a wine list.

'Jenni?'

'Mineral water will be fine. I'm not used to alcohol in the middle of the day,' she explained. A curious expression crossed Nate's face before he closed the list and handed it back to the waiter with a request for two mineral waters.

The food menu appeared more problematic. Most of the dishes were written in French and Jenni's rusty schooldays translations were not up to the mark. Nate helped her translate some of them and pointed out the ones Nathalie had recommended to him.

'You must think I'm a real idiot,' she remarked after they had placed their order and the waiter had departed.

'Why would I think that?' He fiddled about with the stem of his glass, twisting the crystal around.

'Well, I bet you're used to women who often come to this kind of place. You know, fancy menus and all this kind of thing.' She couldn't help noticing the movement of his long supple fingers on the glass. The same hands that had held her so closely just a few hours ago.

'Jenni, some of the women I know who could read that menu could *only* read a menu. In the same way that the only math they can do is in relation to the limit they have on their credit card.' He caught her gaze and held it. 'Don't put yourself down, Jenni. I'm proud to take you anywhere.'

She was glad when the waiter returned with their starters. 'This looks good.' She admired the artistic arrangement of fish on her plate. She had never been anywhere so nice before. Not long before her father's death, her parents had taken her to a steak restaurant as a reward for passing her exams. It had been a rare and unexpected treat. It had been the only time she could ever remember in her life when she'd felt she had succeeded in pleasing them.

'Penny for your thoughts?' Nate watched her, his face thoughtful.

'I was thinking about my parents,' she replied truthfully, 'I was wishing...' Her voice trailed off. 'It isn't important.'

'Whatever you were thinking, it made you look sad, Jen. You have very expressive eyes and I know it wasn't a happy thought.' The note of warm concern in his voice moved her. His perception touched her heart.

'Tell me more about your family,' she said. Although she had known Nate for a long time now, she knew very little about his private life.

Nate took a sip of his mineral water before he answered.

'My father is a surgeon. He's semi-retired now and does mainly private work. Mum is from France, so they go over there quite often.' The main course arrived. He paused until the waiter had gone again before continuing. 'Jerome is two years older than me and Nathalie. He's a photographer. Barnaby is the baby of the family, although at six foot four, he wouldn't thank me for saying so.

He's an artist, like Mum.'

A pang of something like loss resonated through Jenni's heart at Nate's description.

'What about you, Jenni? Do you have any aunts or uncles?'

She shook her head and prodded her trout with the fish knife. 'My parents were both only children. They were in their forties when they adopted me. That's why I wanted to find my birth mother. I don't know who my real father is. It just says *Father Unknown* on my birth certificate. I have so many questions I need answers for.'

The gentle touch of his hand on her cheek made her lift her gaze from the poor fish she had been mindlessly poking on her plate.

'I'm sure you'll get your answers soon, Jenni.'

She swallowed. His tender caress combined with the compassionate tone of his voice rendered her unable to think straight.

'Nate! Jenni! What a nice surprise to see you two here!'

At the sound of his sister's voice, Nate whipped his hand away from Jenni's face as if her skin had burnt his fingers. His abrupt withdrawal left Jenni with a racing heart and her emotions in a whirl.

CHAPTER SIX

'Nathalie, we were just talking about you.' Nate stood up to greet his sister in traditional Gallic fashion, with kisses on both cheeks.

Like Nate, Nathalie was tall, with the same jet black hair. Hers fell in an abundance of curls all the way down to her waist. Dressed in a smart, tailored suit, she looked very glamorous and pretty. Her eyes twinkled at Nate's discomfiture at being caught in an intimate moment with Jenni.

'I do hope my brother isn't working you too hard, Jenni?' Nathalie queried.

Jenni smiled in response. 'Oh no, Nate was very kindly treating me to lunch. He mentioned you had recommended the restaurant here.'

'Well, if Nate took any notice at all of something that I've said, then it's a first. You look fabulous, Jenni. I hardly recognized you.'

'You're welcome to join us if you haven't eaten.' Nate felt obligated to offer, but couldn't help hoping his sister would take a hint and disappear.

'I've eaten already and much as I'd love to, I can't stay. Besides, I'm sure you don't *really* want a gooseberry sitting with you while you eat, do you?'

Nate groaned inwardly while Jenni looked a little embarrassed. After more kisses, his twin departed, leaving a faint trail of perfume in her wake.

Nate resumed his seat opposite Jenni. 'My sister the diplomat,' he joked.

'She seems to have got the wrong impression, seeing us here together.'

'Well, that's Nathalie. She's an incurable romantic. She falls in and out of love like other people take a bath.'

Jenni continued to pick at her fish. 'And you?'

Nate wasn't sure how to answer her. Jenni had never asked him such a personal question before.

'I was in love once.' His voice sounded distant as if it belonged to someone else.

'You never talk about Cerys.'

He couldn't read the expression in Jenni's eyes, but he thought about what she had just said. He had heard the exact same words before from his sister, mother, and the doctor they had sent to see him after the accident. They had meant it as a question, a plea for information. Jenni had made it a simple statement of fact.

'No, I don't.' He kept his answer short, daring her to try and push him so he would have an excuse to end this uncomfortable conversation.

'Are you having dessert?' She changed the course of the conversation so fast he felt wrong-footed.

His knife clattered down onto his plate. 'I think I've lost my appetite.' He knew he shouldn't take his pain out on Jenni, but the mention of Cerys' name always triggered the overpowering sense of anger he kept buried deep within. Sometimes it felt so strong it scared him. Guilt swirled in his conscience that just lately, it was Jenni who'd occupied his thoughts. The idea fueled his irritation.

'I'm not hungry either. Perhaps we should leave.' She placed her cutlery down with careful deliberation.

He summoned the waiter over and dealt with the bill. Once Jenni collected her jacket and they were outside in the cold wintry air, his temper cooled as swiftly as the weather. With his emotions back under control, he apologized.

She surveyed him with a cool expression on her face. 'I shouldn't have asked. It's none of my business.' Her eyes locked with his. For the space of a heartbeat, he thought she might stretch up to kiss him. The need for her understanding gnawed at him like a physical pain. *Could he tell her the truth about the accident?*

'I'd better go home. I've a lot of planning to do if we're going to win the contract to-morrow.' Jenni said.

He unlocked the car, opened the door and waited while she climbed in. As she pulled it shut behind her, he felt sure he saw her hands tremble.

Just one small comment about Cerys had opened up a whole can of worms. '*I was in love once.*' Nate's words resonated in Jenni's head. They had sounded so bleak and desolate.

For a split second she glimpsed the hurt and anger in his eyes. His torment made her see what lay in her own heart, so long unacknowledged. She loved Nate.

She'd fallen in love with a man who would never love her back. A man who still grieved for the woman he'd lost two years ago. Yet, he cared about her. She knew he did. Last night he had even perhaps been *attracted* to her. Sadness washed over her like an unwelcome shower. It would be better to forget about last night. After all, hadn't they both agreed it had been a mistake not to be repeated?

It took her a few moments to register that the scenery outside was not on the route back to her flat. 'Where are we going?'

'Back to my house. Some of the papers you'll need are there. It'll be better if you have them now, rather than tomorrow.' He glanced at her. 'And I need to let Rufus out for a little while. Rose doesn't work Sundays.'

Jenni swallowed hard and nervously moistened the dry skin of her lips. 'You could have asked me first.'

Her nerve endings tingled as she caught the look on his face.

'You seemed preoccupied,' he said. 'And just lately I appear to have developed a severe case of foot in mouth.'

She flushed. 'Well, if you weren't so darn touchy...'

'*I'm* touchy!' He snorted with what sounded like derision.

'Yes. You. Some days it's like tiptoeing through a minefield.' She paused, horror-stricken at the words which had popped out of her mouth. Oh boy, where was her tact and diplomacy when she needed it?

'This has to do with Walker, hasn't it?' He braked sharply as the traffic in front of him slowed without any warning. Jenni jerked forward so that the seatbelt pulled back hard against her ribs.

'You're still mad at me about the Christmas party.'

Jenny looked at him, bewildered. 'No, Nate. This has to do with you.' She folded her arms in defiance. 'You need a break. When the contract is sorted out, you need to take a few days holiday.' She waited for the explosion.

To her surprise, he laughed. 'I couldn't agree more. That's exactly what I intend to do. But I must say it seems rich coming from you, Jen. When did *you* last get away?'

Her hands curled of their own accord into tight little fists. The nails cut into the soft skin of her palms. Nate really could be the most infuriating man on the planet. 'I intend to have some time off soon.'

He lifted an eyebrow in disbelief. 'Really?' he drawled, 'and to which exotic hotspot were you planning to go?'

'I have a lot of things to do at home. For your information, my life doesn't revolve around work.'

He swung the car in through the gates to his house and cut the engine. He swore under his breath and turned in his seat to face her. Jenni faced him square on, even though her heart raced at his black expression.

'Meaning that mine does, I suppose,' he retorted. 'The company doesn't run itself, Jenni.'

'I never said it did, Nate, but that doesn't give you the right to make it an excuse for avoiding life, avoiding love.'

The color leached from his face as her words struck home. She would have given anything to take them back. An oppressive silence hung in the air. His jaw-line tightened and he stormed out of the car. The door slammed shut behind him with a bang which made her flinch.

Nate had already opened the front door of the house. As she scrambled out of the car, she wondered wildly if he would close the door behind him and leave her locked out.

'Nate.' She called his name, desperate to take back the words which had hurt him so much. To explain what she'd meant. Rufus bounced out of the house, his tail beating with happiness at the sight of company. Tentatively, she followed the dog as he turned around and headed back through the front door. Rufus pushed ahead of her and pattered towards the kitchen door which stood wide open.

Nate stood in the kitchen in front of the window, his back towards her. His wide shoulders appeared rigid. He was as still as a statue.

'Nate?'

He half-turned to glance at her as if he had forgotten her existence. He strode to the back door and flung it open. Rufus capered outside into the garden. Nate followed him. Jenni was alone in the kitchen.

Jenni folded her arms to hug herself against the bitter cold coming from the open door. Once Nate was no longer in view she stepped across to close it.

Nate paused in a small grove of trees. The icy air filled his lungs and brought him to a halt. Rufus moped about from tree to tree. The dog stopped from time to time to give Nate a 'what are you doing here?' look as he sniffed at the different scents in the straggly grass. Nate raked his hand through his hair.

'What am I doing here?' he murmured.

Rufus cocked his head to one side as if

waiting for an explanation. Nate sighed. Jenni had a knack for getting under his skin. He had prided himself on how well he'd coped with the aftermath of the accident. He'd refused all the well-intended offers of help and dealt with the pain on his own.

Except he hadn't dealt with it, according to Jenni. He'd avoided it, the same accusation Nathalie had leveled at him. He closed his eyes to try to blot out the memories which threatened to surface and engulf him.

He paced up and down along the path. He had to tell Jenni about Cerys. He knew that now. He just had to choose the right moment to make her see why he couldn't fall in love again. Why he couldn't hope for any woman to love him.

He regained his composure and glanced back towards the house. Jenni no longer stood at the window. Maybe she had called a taxi to go home. Nate couldn't blame her if she had. Rufus answered his whistle, and together they headed back up the path towards the house.

He pushed the kitchen door open to find the room empty. For a split second, it looked as if she'd gone and his stomach contracted in pain at the idea. Then he smelt the delicious aroma of fresh coffee and heard the gentle burbling of his state-of-the-art percolator.

Rufus padded in to settle himself in his dog basket with a mournful look at Nate as if to question his sanity. Jenni came in through the door which led to the hall. She looked uncertain. Without her glasses to hide behind, she appeared more vulnerable than he had ever seen her. A snatch of guilt tugged at his conscience. It had happened again, once more he'd hurt someone he cared about.

'I made some coffee. I thought you might be cold.' She watched him warily, poised in the doorway as if she thought he might order her to leave.

'Thanks, I could use a drink.'

He studied her as she took two mugs from the shelf to pour the drinks.

This new Jenni confused him. The old Jenni would have been half way home in a taxi by now. That Jenni wouldn't have still been here in his kitchen calmly making coffee. In the space of a few days, she had changed so much from the woman he had worked with every day for the last eighteen months. Had he ever really known Jenni? These new-found feelings he had towards her scared him more than he had ever thought possible. Yet how would she react if she knew he had been responsible for Cerys' death?

She passed him a mug of coffee. 'Nate, I should have chosen my words more carefully. I know you find it hard to talk about Cerys and,' she paused, 'well, you're my friend. I care about you.'

Pain welled up inside him and his grip tightened on the handle of his own mug. She saw him as a friend. Why should that hurt so much?

'Forget it, Jenni. It's not a subject I want to discuss.' His voice sounded harsh even to his own ears. He couldn't fail to see her pained expression at his abruptness. 'I know you meant well, though.' He added the last part in a softer tone, as he struggled to keep control of his emotions.

'Well, if you want to run through the other documents with me, then I'll go home and let you finish off your work.' Her voice sounded stiffly businesslike.

He raked his hand through his hair and finished up by rubbing at the sore muscles at the back of his neck. *Soon, he would have to tell her soon.*

'Come through to the office. I'll get the papers.' He kept his voice curt as he walked out past her to lead the way to his study.

Nate pulled up outside Jenni's flat. His eyes narrowed when he noticed the group of teenage boys hanging around the shops near her front door.

'I'll walk you in.' His mouth set in a determined line.

'It's all right, they're always hanging about.' It was quite true. A group of kids always hung about either outside the takeaway or the off license. They left litter and daubed graffiti on her front door. In the summer, when she had her windows open, she could hear them swearing and could smell the smoke from their cigarettes.

'I'm seeing you safely inside. Don't the police ever come and move them on?' he queried.

'All the time, but they keep drifting back.'

She clicked on the stairwell light after she opened the door. Nate bent down to retrieve a folded scrap of lined paper from the vestibule floor.

'Someone's left you a note, Jenni.' He handed the piece of paper over. Puzzled, she glanced at the writing on the front. It just had her name – no address, so someone must have called by and pushed it through the letterbox by hand.

'You should read it upstairs.' Nate suggested with a glance at the audience of teenagers outside the door.

Jenni led the way up to her flat. A cold ominous sensation settled over her.

She dropped her bag onto the floor, then sank down on the settee to unfold the note. Nate stood near her as she scanned the ill-written missive.

'It's from Tracey, my birth mother.' The message seemed confused, almost as if her mother had been in trouble of some kind and had written the note in a hurry.

'I didn't think she had your address?' Nate sounded puzzled, a frown creased his brow.

'She doesn't. At least I've never given it to her. I took your advice about taking it slowly in getting to know her. I didn't put any of my details on the letter I sent to her.' Jenni felt baffled.

'So what does she want?' The harsh tone in Nate's voice made her look at him in some surprise.

'Why would she want anything?' Jenni asked. 'This just says her personal situation is difficult at the moment. She still wants to meet me, but needs to wait a little while until things settle down at home.' She passed the note over. Nate studied it for a few minutes without speaking.

'How did she find out where you live? This whole thing doesn't add up, Jen.'

In her heart, she knew he had a point. Jenni hadn't given her mother her home address. Her adoptive father had always emphasized Tracey's bad character. It might have caused Jenni problems if Tracey had turned up at the flat and they had nothing in common.

'Why do you live here, Jenni?' The question she dreaded hung in the air.

She tried to find an explanation which didn't lay her open to humiliation and pity.

'I moved here when Mum was ill, to be near the nursing home.' She pleated between her fingers the knitted throw which covered the tatty seat.

'And?' he pressed, 'Why haven't you moved? I know you hate this flat. I've seen your face when I bring you home, Jenni.'

She knew Nate would be determined to get to the bottom of the riddle of why she chose to live in such an awful place. He wouldn't let up till he had the answer.

'The nursing home cost me a lot of money. I had to sell Mum and Dad's house. When those funds ran out, I borrowed the money to keep Mum there. I can't afford to move yet, Nate.' Now that she had confessed her money worries to someone, a huge weight lifted from her shoulders. She'd struggled along with it for so long alone.

He stayed silent for a moment. 'Why didn't you tell me? I would have loaned you the money or helped you work something out.'

'I don't want charity, Nate. Making sure Mum was happy and cared for in the place of her choice was the least I could do for her.' She knew her voice sounded sharp and she didn't intend it to. She valued her independence. Her flat might not be very special, but she had paid off most of the debt with her own hard work. Soon she would be able to start getting a deposit together. Then she'd be able to find a new home.

She hadn't been working for Nate very long when her mother had died. Nate had still been wrapped up in his grief for Cerys. Jenni learned from her childhood to be independent, to keep things to herself. Old habits died hard.

'So what are you going to do now?'

Jenni blinked. 'Do?'

'Now your birth mother has your address?' He tapped the note between his fingers. 'Reading between the lines, it sounds as if she might be involved with something or someone pretty unsavory.'

Jenni stared at him. 'Surely not. Maybe she simply has a lot on at the moment. We don't know anything about her life. It *is* almost Christmas.'

Nate frowned. 'Exactly. You don't know anything about her. You didn't give her your address, so how did she find you? I'm sorry, Jen. I'm concerned about you, that's all. I think you're too vulnerable living here by yourself.'

'There must be a simpler explanation, Nate.' She became aware of the faint pleading note in her voice. She hadn't realized until now just how much she wanted everything to be all right, to have someone who belonged to her. Someone who was truly family. How pathetic was that? Nate scowled, his face perplexed.

'Yes, there probably is.' The small crease stayed on his forehead as he handed the note back to her.

He looked at his watch and grimaced. 'I have to go, Jenni. I'll pick you up in the morning and give you a lift into work. Promise me you'll take extra care about your security. Don't answer the door if you don't know who it is.'

'I'm not a child, Nate. I've lived here on my own for over a year now, I think I can take care of myself.' She resented the implication that she couldn't be trusted to take basic safety precautions.

'Just be careful, Jenni. I'll pick you up at seven, which should give us time to get quite a lot of work done before the rest of the staff arrives for briefing.'

She followed him to the door. 'Okay I'll see you tomorrow.'

He paused at the top of the stairs, his expression serious as he surveyed her face. 'Lock the door behind me, Jenni.'

Something about the set of his shoulders made her heart beat a little faster. The butterflies started to dance in her stomach. 'I will.'

CHAPTER SEVEN

Jenni dressed the next morning with special care. She decided to wear one of the new tailored suits Lorna had persuaded her to buy. The department store on the high street had been having a pre-Christmas special sale, so she had managed to buy two outfits for the price of what one would normally have cost her. The amount she'd saved appealed to her bank balance. The fit of the suit appealed to her vanity.

The morning flew by. The team from New York arrived and appeared to be impressed with both the model of the planned building and the presentation. The brunch she arranged went well too. By mid-afternoon, the clients left to go back to their hotel to rest. Jenni took the opportunity to clear up while Nate debriefed the rest of the team.

She and Nate had been invited to dine with Mr. Woods, the head of the delegation, and his P.A., at their hotel that evening before they left for London in the morning to see the rival bid.

'This is our chance to really show what we can do,' Nate told Jenni as she gathered up the briefing papers in the boardroom. 'Mr. Woods is very particular about the companies he works with. It's not only having a great design. He always says he likes to feel a rapport with the people he employs. That's why he's here and not some junior executive. If it all goes well tonight, we might just seal the deal.'

Jenni paused in her tidying. 'So, how well do you think we're doing?'

'He seemed to love everything so far about the quality of the project and he was quite amenable to the suggestions we put to him,' Nate said.

'But?' Jenni asked.

Nate sighed. 'I don't know. I have a feeling the real decider will be the dinner tonight. After all, today we only went over the things that must have already been pitched to him in New York.'

Jenni's confidence plummeted. She wasn't good at social small talk. What if she messed the deal up tonight for Nate? Miss Marchant, the American P.A, or Jo, as she had said she preferred to be called, had looked very pleasant, but appeared very sophisticated to Jenni. Her conversation had been peppered with quotes like, 'When we were in New Zealand,' 'When we did the Japanese project' and 'When we were in Hungary.' Jenni hadn't even traveled as far as London very often. How could she compete?

'Why don't you ask Nathalie to go to the dinner tonight? She's very good at making conversation, I'm sure she'd do a better job of selling the contract.' All Jenni could think about was how terrible she'd feel if they lost the contract because of her social ineptitude. Nathalie was a successful businesswoman in her own right, she would be sure to make a good impression.

Nate stared at her with a frown. 'Why would I want to ask Nathalie? You're my P.A. You know more about the project than most people. You've done a terrific job here today.'

Jenni flushed. 'I just thought...' she faltered. Nate gazed at her, obviously baffled.

'Jenni, I have every faith in you. There is nothing for you to worry about. Just treat tonight as a pleasant night out.'

She shuffled the papers in her hands into a folder, intent on her task. The touch of his hands on her shoulders as he came to stand behind her startled her and sent a thrill of anticipation through her body.

'Just be yourself, Jenni. You'll be fine.'

The phone rang. He took his hands from her shoulders as she reached across to take the call.

Back in her bedroom after a long luxurious soak in the bath, Jenni surveyed the contents of her wardrobe in despair. What did you wear to a meal in a five star hotel restaurant? Thanks to Lorna, she had a respectable work wardrobe and even a couple of new casual things, but anything more formal became a struggle.

Gloomily, she studied her options. A black dress she had worn for her mother's funeral. A pink summer strappy dress she had worn for a college friend's wedding years ago, or a very clingy cherry red dress Lorna had given her a few months ago.

She pulled the red dress out of the closet. It had been one of Lorna's impulse buys from a shop that had been closing down. On getting it home, she had discovered it didn't fit her and had gifted it to Jenni. Jenni had never envisaged herself at the time as being brave enough to wear it. Perhaps now was the time to get her courage up.

She stared at it for a few more minutes, then looked again at her other choices. A picture of Jo Marchant looking immaculate in a beautiful evening dress flashed through her head. She knew she had no option but to brazen it out in the red dress.

By the time Nate rang her doorbell at precisely eight o'clock, the butterflies in her stomach had been replaced by elephants with wings. It would be difficult to eat a three-course dinner when she felt as sick as a dog. Her confidence had grown since she had started to work for Nate. However, the importance he'd attached to this occasion had sent her right back to square one. She hated to feel uncertain, so paused for a moment to collect her thoughts before she hurried down the stairs to let Nate in.

Jenni's mouth gaped open when she opened the door. He wore a tailored black suit she hadn't seen before. As he stood on her doorstep, he looked larger, darker, and more handsome than ever. His eyes widened as he took in her appearance. A low whistle left his lips.

'Wow Jenni! You look fantastic.'

This time there could be no doubt about his opinion of her image. He studied her with open admiration. 'You'll knock them dead.'

Her pulse still beat wildly as she checked in her coat at the hotel cloakroom. She took her place next to Nate in the lobby and looked around for their hosts.

The elevator doors opened. The Americans appeared. Jo Marchant looked resplendent in an oriental jade silk two-piece suit. Nate gave Jenni's hand a quick comforting squeeze. She savored the brief touch and drew strength from the fleeting contact.

To her relief, the meal went well. Mr. Woods, or Sam as he rapidly became, was a genial and entertaining host. Jo Marchant proved to be an educated, interesting hostess. The part Jenni had been dreading, making casual conversation, had been fun after all.

After coffee, Sam suggested they adjourn to the residents' lounge for a post-dinner liqueur. Jenni excused herself to go to the powder room. Jo accompanied her. They walked across the marble tiled floor of the lobby together.

Jenni stood in front of the marble-topped basins and ran cool water over her hot wrists. She stole a quick glance at Jo as she touched up her lipstick. The American girl appeared well groomed, sophisticated, with not a hair out of place.

'I hope you don't mind my asking a personal question,' Jo said, 'but you and Nate? Are you an item?' She looked at Jenni.

Jenni paused. A great spear of jealousy pierced her heart. She wished she could lie. 'No, we're not. Nate's fiancée was killed in an accident two years ago. We're just friends and colleagues.' She hoped she sounded calm and matter-of-fact.

'Mmm, I see. That must have been terrible for him.'

'He doesn't like to talk about it.' Jenni's dismay grew as she watched Jo. If anyone was elegant, intelligent and beautiful enough to replace Cerys in Nate's affections, then Jo stood a good chance. Jenni's green-eyed jealousy monster raged inside her. Each word Jo spoke was a fresh stab of anguish.

Jo smiled. 'Two years is a long time alone for a guy as good looking as Nate. I can't believe he doesn't date.'

'He loved Cerys very much.' Jenni felt compelled to defend him.

'Maybe he needs to meet the right woman.' Jo suggested. She smoothed her already perfect hair. The iron bands around Jenni's heart tightened as she fiddled with her watch to hide her agitation. She hoped Jo hadn't noticed her hands tremble on the strap.

The rest of the night passed in pure agony for Jenni. Jo's technique was subtle. Jenni had to give her credit for that. There was no

123

out-and-out flirting, just solicitous attention to his every word. Pain twisted like a dagger in Jenni's heart every time Nate responded.

Jenni remained lost in her own thoughts and oblivious of her silence until Sam spoke. 'Are you tired, Jenni? It's been a busy day.'

'I am, actually. It's been a great evening and a real pleasure to get to know you both but I think I'd better call it a night.' She picked up her bag and stood up. Nate leapt to his feet.

'I'll take a taxi home, Nate. I don't want to be the party pooper.' She smiled apologetically at Sam and Jo.

'No, I'll take you home. It's late. This close to Christmas, it can be difficult to get a cab.' Nate offered.

A sneaky part of her was glad he didn't want to stay with Jo, but she couldn't help feeling concerned the Americans might be offended if they both disappeared.

'Actually, Jo and I are ready to call it a night, too. We've that trip to London tomorrow. It's been a busy day today. I think the old jet lag is creeping in.' Sam shook hands with Nate and kissed Jenni on the cheek. 'It's been a great night. I'll be in touch soon. Good to get to know you both.'

The roads gleamed white with frost when

they left the hotel. Ice covered the Range Rover. Jenni huddled up in the front of the car while Nate ran the engine to defrost the windows.

'That went well, don't you think?' she asked as Nate cleared the windscreen.

'Not bad. You were great. Sam is a bit old-fashioned when it comes to business. He always prefers to deal with people he feels he knows and he claims that by meeting people in a less formal setting, he can soon tell which companies he would be happy to deal with.'

'Is he right?' Jenni asked. 'Has he ever had his fingers burned?'

Nate laughed. 'No, Sam Woods is a shrewd judge of people. He always seems to do well with his developments. Once Sam has your company on his team, he puts lots of contracts your way. That's why tonight was so important.'

'I see.' She longed to ask him what he thought of Jo Marchant, but, then again, did she really want to know?

Her mind ran back over the conversation she'd had with Jo. The other girl had much more in common with Nate than she did. Jo was everything she imagined Cerys to have been. Jenni sighed. The more she thought about it, the more depressed she felt. Maybe she had been fooling herself when she'd thought Nate was attracted to her. A make-over and new clothes might not be enough to make him see her for the woman she really was.

The pavement outside Jenni's flat looked deserted for once, it being too cold even for the gang of teenage diehards. Nate turned towards her.

'Thank you for everything today, Jenni. You've been fantastic. You kept everybody and everything running like clockwork.' His warm voice rang with approval.

'No problem, truly. I know how much the contract means to you.' Her spirits lifted again at his praise.

He lifted his hand to stroke a stray tendril of her hair and curled it idly around his finger. 'In case I didn't tell you, you looked fabulous tonight, Jenni.'

The blood rushed in her ears as her pulse moved up another notch. As if from a distance, she heard a squeaky 'Oh' come out of her mouth right before he kissed her.

Rufus greeted him with unabashed relief on his return home and bounced up the hall to drop a half-chewed dog biscuit at Nate's feet. He sank down into a nearby armchair to rub the top of Rufus's silky head as he turned the events of the night over in his mind.

Jenni didn't stray too far from his thoughts as he remembered her in that fantastic red dress with the fabric that clung to her slender curves as she walked on her high heels – a beautiful young woman who oozed sex appeal and unconscious charm. The woman he'd kissed till they had both been breathless with passion. Someone he had no right to love.

While the girls had been in the powder room, Sam Woods had told him how impressed he had been by Jenni both in and out of the office.

'You're a lucky man, Nate!' Sam had remarked, as he'd puffed on his cigar.

The deep shameful sense that he had betrayed Cerys' memory filled his soul. He realized for twenty-four hours now, he hadn't thought of Cerys. Hadn't compared other women to her, hadn't smelled her perfume or glimpsed a girl who looked enough like her to compel him to turn around to check the impossible. What had happened to him?

It had to be Jenni, but she deserved love, deserved a man who could give her his whole heart. Not someone like him. A man whose heart was buried with another woman in a cold and lonely grave. Nate had forfeited all rights to fall in love again the night he had failed Cerys.

Jenni wasn't sure what to expect from Nate when she arrived for work the next morning. He had looked at her after they'd kissed as if he hadn't known who she was. He had recoiled from her so fast it had been embarrassing. She had to face the truth – no matter how much she might try to reach it. Cerys still held Nate's heart.

Bitterly, she almost wished Jo Marchant luck. Almost, because she still had a niggling doubt that Jo might succeed where Jenni had failed.

Mike Walker waited by Lorna's desk as Jenni arrived. She smiled at him distractedly. In the last few days he had been hanging around a lot.

'Wow, Jenni, you look fabulous. I wanted to tell you yesterday, but I was so busy.' His eyes gleamed with frank admiration from behind his glasses.

'Thank you, Mike.' Something in her tone caused Lorna to look at her with a frown. Mike continued to loiter. He joined in the discussion whenever the opportunity arose. Jenni wished he wouldn't stand so close to her.

'When you've quite finished swapping gossip, Jennifer, we do have a business to run. Mr Walker, I'm sure there are plenty of things to do in your department.'

Jenni swivelled on her heels, Nate never called her Jennifer. Her temper heated when she tilted her head upward to look at his face.

CHAPTER EIGHT

Mike disappeared towards the lift. Lorna found a pressing errand to run. Which left Nate and Jenni alone by the reception desk.

'That was uncalled for, Nate.' Jenni's heart thumped wildly at his closeness.

'Maybe, but there seems to be too much time wasted in idle gossiping around here lately. I know everyone is getting tired and it's almost Christmas, but I still have a business to run.' He glowered at her as if he expected her to put up an argument.

'In that case then, I'll collect the mail and make a start,' she answered.

'I take it everything's ready for the party next week?'

Jenni took a deep breath, struggling to keep her cool. He knew very well she had prepared everything.

'Of course, I ran everything past you a few weeks ago, I'm sure you remember,' she said pointedly. 'Now is there anything else or shall I get started?'

He looked as though he was about to try

to think of something else, as he scowled at her. She was relieved when the phone rang. With Lorna still not back, Jenni grabbed it like a lifeline.

'Mayer Holdings, may I help you?' She half-turned to lean over the desk to reach for a notepad. She struggled to hear the faint female voice on the line. The woman spoke quietly almost as if she didn't want to be overheard. It was difficult to understand her.

'I would like to speak to Jennifer Blake, please.'

Jenni didn't recognize the voice, but that wasn't unusual. 'Speaking, can I help you?'

'This is Tracey, I sent you a note the other day?'

Nate stepped to her side so he could hear the conversation, alerted by the tone of her voice.

'Yes, I got it. You said things were difficult for you at the moment.' Jenni shook with fear. She crossed the fingers of her free hand behind her back. It would be awful if her mother had called to say she didn't want any further contact.

'I can't see you until after Christmas. It's too difficult for me. I don't want you to have any bother...' Tracey was almost whispering. Jenni could barely hear her. 'I'll get in touch

132

as soon as it's safe. I ... he's coming back, I have to go.' Before Jenni had a chance to respond, the line went dead. She stared at the receiver.

Nate took the phone from her and placed the handset back in the cradle.

'Was it Tracey?' he asked.

Jenni's mind whirled. It had sounded as if her birth mother was frightened of someone – and frightened for Jenni. What could be going on? She blinked back her tears.

'Come on, we'll talk about this upstairs.' Nate slipped a gentle, yet protective arm around her shoulders, and steered her towards the lift.

'What did she say?' Nate's deep voice rumbled in her ear. Inside the privacy of his office, he stepped away from her and stood with his hands in his pockets, watching her.

She repeated the conversation to Nate word-for-word.

'What do you think?' she asked.

To her dismay, he didn't give her an immediate answer. In fact, she sensed him almost struggling with himself – as if he knew or suspected something she didn't.

'Well?' she demanded, after a couple of silent and awkward minutes had ticked by.

'I didn't want to tell you this, because I

133

knew you wouldn't like it and would probably tell me to mind my own business.' He
paused, as if to weigh up how she might
receive what he was about to say.

'What are you talking about?' Today had
turned into a bad dream. Perhaps if she
pinched herself she might wake up.

'I was worried for your safety after the note
got pushed through your door, so I engaged
a private investigator to do some research.'

Indignation at his actions fought with fear
for her mother's safety. 'You did what?' she
managed eventually.

'I was concerned about how she might have
got hold of your home address and why the
note had been left there rather than posted
here. I think she's mixed up in something,
Jenni, and on one point I wholly agree with
her. I don't want you involved with it either.'

Dumbfounded, she looked at him. The
impact of his words seeped into her sub-
conscious. Her teeth chattered as a wave of
nausea washed over her.

Strong arms held her tight and a man's
voice murmured reassurance in her ear. A
deep familiar voice. Nate.

Dazed, she opened her eyes. 'I never faint,'
she protested.

'For someone who never faints, you make

quite a habit of it,' he remarked.

She pushed herself up into a sitting position, taking care not to hurry. The physical exertion made the blood rush back into her head. Nate steadied her against his chest.

'Stay still until the dizziness wears off,' he advised.

'I'm okay now, really.' She wasn't sure if it was the faint or Nate that made her head feel muzzy.

He pulled out his office chair and made her sit down on it.

'I just panicked. It all seemed so extraordinary. A bit like an episode from a TV drama.' The scenarios she had created in her mind rushed back to her, making her stomach knot.

Nate leaned against the desk in front of her, his brow creased in thought. 'I haven't had much back yet, Jenni, but what the investigator has discovered so far indicates Tracey herself doesn't seem to be involved in anything shifty.'

'But...' Jenni said, confused. There had to be something more.

'The man she's living with is another kettle of fish altogether. Apparently, he has a criminal record as long as your arm, and it's not small stuff.'

Jenni digested the information in silence for a moment. The whole thing sounded so incredible. 'Do you think Tracey is in any danger?'

'I don't know. I presume she knows all about this man. She seems aware of the risks she's running. Why else would she ring you?'

'Why would it involve me in any kind of danger?'

Nate shrugged. 'I'm not sure. All I can think is that he doesn't like Tracey contacting you. Perhaps he's afraid of you poking around asking awkward questions. It does worry me that he knows where you live.'

Jenni shivered. 'Should I go to the police?'

Nate scratched his chin, deep in thought. 'I don't think it would do any good. We've nothing definite to go on. We'll know more in a few days' time when the investigator has finished his research.'

A chill of fear ran up Jenni's spine. 'What shall I do until then?' It felt frightening when she thought of being on her own in her flat. Not knowing who might be watching or waiting for her. For all she knew he could be spying on her right now...

Nate sighed. Today was not going to plan at all. He had intended to place his friendship with Jenni back onto a more formal footing. But when she'd been so close, he wanted to hold her tight against him and kiss her fears away. That definitely *wasn't* part of the plan.

He wasn't sure what Jenni should do – he didn't want to cause her unnecessary alarm. All the same, he didn't like the idea of her going home. It made her too vulnerable living there already without any extra threat to her safety.

'How long do you think it'll be before the detective finds out anything more definite?'

He could see the fear in her beautiful blue eyes – eyes that trusted him to protect her.

The same look that had been in Cerys' eyes.

Nate took a deep breath, fighting to drag air into lungs which had forgotten how to breathe. His fists clenched into white-knuckled balls with the effort, and a cold trail of sweat trickled down his spine.

'He was hoping to have something by next week.' Nate forced himself to sound calm.

'What am I going to do?'

Her voice held a note of despair. Nate gritted his teeth.

'Stay at my house for tonight. You'll be fine there. Tomorrow I'll try to find out more.' He swallowed hard and prayed he had done the right thing.

Jenni looked at him. He knew what few options were available to her were being considered.

'Nate, I couldn't impose on you like that. For all we know we might have the whole thing blown right out of proportion.'

'Do you want to go back to your flat? Stay on your own? Unless you want me to spend the night on your couch, I suggest you stay at my house for tonight.'

She nodded. 'Okay, but I'll have to collect some things from home.'

'We'll stop by after work and you can pack your toothbrush.' At last she'd seen sense.

'Thanks for doing this, Nate.' She stood up and crossed over to the office door. 'I'd better go back to work.'

Jenni closed the door behind her as she left Nate's office. Why had her life become so complicated?

Nate being around her all the time for the next few days wasn't going to be simple. He would be horrified if he found out she had fallen in love with him. She could lose everything she valued most – her job, her home, and most importantly, Nate.

It was dark. Almost everyone else had

gone home by the time she finished the last letter in her in-tray. She switched off her computer with a sigh of relief, then got up to tap on Nate's door.

She opened it a crack and saw he was deep in conversation on the telephone. She had decided to creep out again when he noticed her. Jenni waited by the door until he finished his conversation and hung up the phone.

'That was Sam Woods. We did it. We've won the contract.' A broad smile lit up Nate's face. Jenni grinned back, delighted with their success.

'That's fantastic, Nate. You deserve it.'

Nate advanced across the room. He picked her up and swung her around. 'No, we deserve it,' he corrected her when he set her down on her feet again.

She felt a little giddy. 'It was your design. I told you it was wonderful.'

His hands still encircled her waist. She felt his warmth through the thin silky material of her blouse. Shakily, she took a small step away from him, her head turned away so he couldn't see her rosy face.

'We'd better go. The cleaners will be here in a minute. I need to go home and pack a bag.' She hoped she sounded breezy and un-concerned. One touch from Nate reduced her to jelly. She didn't think her acting skills were up to fooling him.

Jenni's stomach rolled with a sick nervousness as they pulled up outside Nate's house. She hoped Nate's housekeeper wouldn't be in. What would the woman think if she saw Jenni arrive with her overnight bag? She called a halt to her thoughts. It was crazy to keep comparing her life now to the one she'd lived under her parents' roof. She was a grown woman, a free agent. There was no need for her to be scared of people's opinions any more.

Fortunately, from Jenni's point of view, the only resident at home was Rufus. The dog greeted them both with equal delight. She followed Nate into the house and waited in the hall for him to tell her where she could leave her bag.

'I'll show you where everything is. Then I'll make some tea while you unpack.' Nate's hunched shoulders indicated he was as uncomfortable as she felt. He showed her into a pretty, spacious room just off the first floor landing.

'The bathroom is through there. Make yourself at home, Jen. If you want anything, just help yourself.'

She looked around at the comfortable

bedroom, with its restful cream and green color scheme. 'This is lovely Nate – thank you. I don't know what I would have done if you hadn't invited me to stay here.'

He looked a little irritated by her thanks. 'You're welcome. I'll put the kettle on. Come down when you're ready.'

Jenni took a few minutes to unpack her things and freshen up. After a few deep breaths to calm her nerves, and a touch up of her lipstick, she made her way back to the kitchen.

'Rose has left a lamb casserole for us.' Nate handed her a mug of tea.

'That's very kind of her. Can I do anything to help?'

'No, it's all ready. Have a seat and I'll dish up.'

She sat down at one end of the long beech table where he had set a place. Nate slid the dish from the oven and began to ladle the rich meat casserole onto a plate. His shoulders sloped with fatigue. Her heart clenched with sympathy.

He sat down opposite her and began to eat. Jenni wondered if he'd eaten much lunch. If she hadn't gone out and fetched him a sandwich, he probably wouldn't have eaten all day.

'Are you alright, Nate? You seem to have a lot on your mind.'

'Sorry, I was miles away.' He picked at the casserole on his plate.

'You don't seem very hungry.'

'I'm just tired, I guess.'

Nate looked far too attractive sitting there at the end of the table. He had taken off his tie and loosened the collar of his shirt. A faint black shadow of beard covered his jaw.

She shifted on her seat and wondered what was on his mind. A couple of times she thought he was about to speak. It could be so nice. To come home together at the end of the day, share a meal, chat. Tension fizzed in the air. Jenni sensed the grounds of their relationship had shifted.

'I wish we knew more about what was happening with Tracey.'

'We should know a little more about Tracey's situation tomorrow.' Nate stood up and stacked his plate in the dishwasher. 'I'm going up to take a shower. Help yourself to anything you need. If you want to go and watch television or anything, feel free.'

'I will. Thank you.' He looked at her for a moment as if he was about to say something else, but turned instead and left the room. After a few minutes, Jenni abandoned her pretense at eating and scraped the remnants from her plate into the bin before placing it in the dishwasher and going through to the lounge.

She switched on the lamps before she crossed over to the window to draw the curtains. She hadn't been in this room yet, except to open the door when she had been looking for the cloakroom on Sunday afternoon. A large bookcase stood to one side of the fireplace. She went over to take a look, thinking a book might occupy her mind and help her to sleep.

A small photograph in a simple silver frame stood close to the edge on the far corner of the top shelf, half-turned so that it faced the wall. Jenni didn't need to be told who it was. She looked at the face of the woman she had heard so much about but had never seen.

Nate had no pictures of Cerys in his office. Until now, Jenni hadn't seen any in his home. Absorbed in her thoughts, she didn't hear the door click open or Nate enter the room. Mortified at being caught with the photograph in her hands, she fumbled with the frame trying to stand it back up on the shelf.

'I'm sorry, I didn't mean, I was after a book...'

Nate's attention stayed fixed on the photograph, his expression grimmer and bleaker than she had ever seen. She knew the picture had brought back the past and his memories. Her breath caught in her throat.

'Nate...' Her voice came out as a husky croak.

'I'd almost forgotten that was still there.' His speech slowed as though it cost a physical effort for him to force the words from his lips.

Jenni lifted her hand from the picture, her eyes still fixed on his face. Nate sank down on the nearby armchair and buried his face in his hands. To her horror his shoulders started to shake as he struggled to contain his grief.

Unable to stop herself, she moved to his side and placed a tentative hand on his shoulder as she knelt on the floor beside him.

'You need to let her go, Nate.' Jenni's heart tore in two as she watched the man she loved grieve over the fiancée who had been lost to him for so long.

'It's not that easy, Jenni,' he said, 'you don't understand. I wanted to tell you, to explain.'

She swallowed hard. 'I know you loved her.'

'I killed her, Jenni.'

She stared at him in disbelief. 'It was an

accident, Nate. There was black ice on the road.'

He lifted his head and met her gaze with tear filled eyes. 'I was responsible. It was my fault.'

Jenni was convinced he had taken leave of his senses. He rubbed his face with weary hands, as though trying to clear his head.

'I've never told anyone what happened that night.'

'But the police report cleared you of any blame. The accident investigator agreed.' Jenni shook her head, desperate to make sense of it all.

'I wasn't the driver that night. Cerys was the one behind the wheel.'

'That's impossible.' Jenni blurted the words out before she could stop herself.

He sighed, 'To understand, Jenni, you have to know what Cerys was like. She tried so hard to be perfect. All her life she tried to please everyone. The perfect daughter, the perfect friend, the perfect fiancée. She spent a fortune on her clothes and her hair. She always wanted to be seen at what she thought were the right places and to be in the right social circles.' His brow darkened with pain.

'She had a group of friends, "the crowd" she called them. I never cared for them very much. They seemed loud and superficial, but they were important to her. They had parties most weekends, and we used to go.' Nate stumbled over the last few words before stopping to rub his face again.

'Cerys tried so hard to be everything to everybody, I didn't realize for a long time that she had serious problems. She hid it so well. She insisted the pills I kept finding were for headaches and it wasn't until she got careless that I started finding the empty vodka bottles. She'd hide them in all kinds of places.'

Jenni's head reeled. 'No one else knew?'

Nate shook his head. 'Only me. She swore she'd get help. That she'd given up. She couldn't bear the thought that anyone might find out. There were so many lies, so many broken promises.' His face looked ashen in the lamplight. She could only guess at the effort sharing this terrible secret had cost him. She took his icy hand between hers as if she could physically save him from his past and revive him with the warmth of her touch.

'The night of the crash, Cerys was at the wheel. I'd discovered she'd been drinking again and threatened to leave her. She hadn't kept the appointments with her therapist.' He swallowed hard. 'We argued. She knew I wouldn't let her drive if she'd been drinking, so she took the keys from my jacket. I jumped in the passenger seat just as she pulled away. That's why neither of us had seatbelts on.'

Jenni saw him relive the nightmare, the scene that tormented him. The stern lines of his mouth wavered and he gripped her hand as if she were the lifeline that would be his salvation.

'She hit a patch of black ice and the car started to spin. Cerys screamed. I grabbed the wheel and tried to correct it, but I couldn't make the turn in time. We hit the tree full on.'

'There wasn't anything you could have done. It wasn't your fault.' Jenni's heart broke afresh with pain for the man she loved.

'I should have stopped her, made her go for her treatment. If I hadn't threatened to leave her, she would never have taken the keys. When the police came to see me afterwards, they didn't know who had been driving because the crash had piled us both up in the front of the car. I felt I owed it to Cerys to protect her memory. For her sake and her parents. They were elderly and doted on her. She was all they had.'

Jenni longed to hold him close and take some of the burden he had carried alone for so long. 'You loved her so much,' she whispered, 'but you didn't kill her, Nate. She made those choices for herself. You did everything you could to protect her, to get her to go for help. You weren't to know she would try to drive that night.' She stroked his cheek and tried to make him see the truth of her words.

He closed his hand over hers, stilling the movement of her fingers. He gazed at her for what seemed like a lifetime, revealing all the shadows and torments of his past before his lips touched hers.

She closed her eyelids as his lips brushed her mouth with the tender sweetness of a vow. In abandoning herself to his kiss she hadn't realized her cheeks were wet with tears until he smoothed them away with the pad of his thumbs.

She opened her eyes again and rose jerkily to her feet. 'You couldn't have done anything more for her, Nate. To get well, she had to want to do that for herself. You can't carry on punishing yourself for something you couldn't prevent.'

He didn't answer for what seemed like a long time, before giving her hand a gentle squeeze. 'Good night, Jenni.'

He had dismissed her. Her heart still

troubled, she left him alone with his thoughts and trudged upstairs to her single room.

The next morning Nate's housekeeper had bustled in and taken off her coat in the kitchen before he got downstairs.

'Morning Nate, you look as if you've had a rough night. Bacon and eggs do you?' Rose opened the fridge to inspect the contents.

'There's an extra person for breakfast this morning, Rose.' Nate had forgotten about Rose arriving early. He had been confident he and Jenni would have left for work before she arrived. Then he would have been able to avoid the speculation Jenni's stay would excite. He could have talked things over with her before they left for work.

'Oh? Will they want bacon and eggs as well?' Rose looked thrilled. She knew Nate hadn't had anyone stay at the house for a long time.

'I'm not sure. She'll be down in a minute I expect.' He busied himself with the coffee-pot. Rose's eyebrows rose a good inch at his remark and her cheery face acquired a flushed, interested look.

'Will the young lady be staying tonight as well? I'll need to buy more groceries.'

149

Nate shot her a glance. He knew Rose's attempts of old to fish for more information. 'I'm not sure. I'm planning to go to the cottage for a few days, so I'd like you to order some groceries in for that.'

'For just you? Or will you be having guests?' Her cheeks glowed pinker than ever and dimpled with mischief.

Jenni slipped into the room. 'I'm sorry, I didn't hear – oh!'

'Rose, this is Jenni, my secretary. Jenni, this is Rose, my housekeeper. Jenni has a problem with her flat so she stayed here overnight.' He watched as the two women appraised each other.

Rose must have approved, because she gave Jenni a cheerful smile and said, 'Sit yourself down, I'll cook you some bacon and eggs.'

If the atmosphere between Nate and Jenni appeared a little constrained, Rose didn't appear to notice. She served them both with breakfast and asked Nate what he wanted to take to the cottage.

Nate only half-heard Rose's questions, his attention was given over to Jenni, whose cheeks had gone as white as the milk in the jug on the table.

CHAPTER NINE

Panic gripped Jenni's heart. Why had Rose asked Nate about his holiday cottage? He hadn't mentioned anything to her last night. If he went away now, and it wasn't safe for her to go home yet, then what was she going to do? She hadn't realized till now how much she had counted on his support.

'I won't leave you in the lurch, Jenni,' he murmured while Rose occupied herself with the frying pan on the other side of the kitchen.

'But what if I can't go home?' Jenni blurted her fear out, unable to stop the panic rising inside her.

'Then you'll have to come with me.'

She looked at him, expecting him to be joking, but his face remained serious. 'I couldn't. What about work?'

'It's only for a few days, and anyway, things are winding down ready for the dance on Saturday. The contract with Sam won't start till the New Year. I think the company can manage without us for a little while.'

'Maybe the detective will say everything is fine and I'll be able to go home.' She tried to sound positive, but Nate just raised an eyebrow at her.

She continued in a hopeful voice. 'It could be that we've blown this out of all proportion.'

'And the moon is made of green cheese and I'm related to Mickey Mouse,' Nate replied.

They stopped at the supermarket on the way, and Nate bought bottles of champagne to greet the staff when they arrived for work, in celebration of the new contract.

The staff soon assembled. A buzz of excitement filled the air in the boardroom as Nate made the announcement and popped the corks on the bottles.

In the midst of the hubbub and chatter, Nate drew Jenni to one side. 'I rang Mr. Field, the detective. He's coming in to see us at lunchtime.'

Jenni bit her lip. Nate smiled at her and squeezed her cold hand. 'At least we'll know what's going on, and if Tracey's alright.'

'I suppose so.' Jenni's worries about her birth mother had been increasing since breakfast.

Mr. Field arrived right on time at twelve

o'clock. A dry little man with a rather sad expression, he wasn't at all how Jenni had imagined a private detective to look. He sat down, looked a little sorrowfully in Jenni's direction, and began his report.

It quickly became clear that Tracey's only crime had been her appalling judgment in men. Her past relationships sounded like one long list of disasters, culminating in Pete, her current partner. The police knew the man sharing her life and her home well. The records reported him to be a drug addict with a psychopathic personality, which took the form of exerting complete control over anyone he was involved with. He had no record of ever harming Tracey, but had threatened or driven off her friends and neighbors, and had convictions for assaulting other people.

Jenni listened in numbed disbelief as Mr. Field recited a list of convictions stretching back over twenty years in his dry little voice.

'Do you think my mother is in any danger?' Jenni asked as the detective rose to leave. Her anxiety must have shown on her face, for his dour expression softened. He shook his head.

'Not at the moment. However, I think you would be wise to heed Mr. Mayer's advice

153

and lie low for a while. Your mother's boy-friend is highly irrational. He believes anyone your mother may be emotionally attached to is a threat to his relationship with her. He may use violence to protect his interests.'

A sudden tremor ran through her body. Nate slipped his arm around her waist. His touch comforted and reassured her. Mr. Field replaced his hat, wished them a happy Christmas without any hint of irony and left.

'Why did I try to find her? Why? My father warned me. Oh Nate, what am I going to do?'

Nate had asked himself the same question.

'I think you should do as Mr. Field suggested. Lie low. Come away with me for a few days. You need the holiday as much as I do.' He thought fast. He couldn't leave Jenni on her own. She had nowhere else to go. She had already confessed she had no money to pay for a hotel, and he knew her streak of stubborn pride would make her refuse any suggestion of a loan.

'It's very generous of you to offer, Nate, but I'm sure there must be...'

He interrupted her before she could finish her sentence. 'Jenni, be realistic. In Devon you'll be far enough away to feel safe. If you stay anywhere in the locality, you could be traced.'

She looked at him, her expression anxious. He could see her trying to think of another solution. For some reason her hesitancy about accepting his invitation irritated him.

'You're coming, Jenni, and that's final. We'll finish off here. I'll drive you home so you can pack.'

Her eyes flashed. 'There must be another solution.'

'I'm not debating this any more, Jenni.'

Jenni looked at him again. He read the mixture of hurt and fear on her expressive face and almost reached for her. To hold her close, smooth her beautiful silky hair and whisper reassurance to her.

Almost.

Jenni fumed to herself all the way to her flat. She knew deep down she had no other option than to go with Nate to his holiday home. If one night in the same house as him had been tortuous enough, this would stretch her beyond belief.

To be alone with Nate in a small cottage beside the sea should have been paradise, except she knew he didn't really want her company. He had insisted on bringing her with him because being the kind of man he was. He'd felt he had no other option.

Jenni didn't want to be an honorable obligation, not to the man she loved.

Rose packed enough food for an army. By the time the Range Rover had been loaded with the food, bags, dog equipment and Rufus, the sun had started to sink in the late afternoon sky.

Nate selected an easy listening station on the car radio as they joined the motorway. Jenni gazed out of the window at the darkening countryside with interest. She hadn't been to the seaside since her last year at college, when there had been a day trip to Blackpool. Her spirits rose. She loved the sea, and her watercolor pad and paints had been tucked into her travel bag alongside her clothes.

'We'll stop off halfway. Rufus will need the exercise.'

They stopped at one of the many motorway services. While Nate took Rufus for a short walk, Jenni wandered around the shop. The range of things they sold amazed her and by the time she rejoined Nate at the car, she had a carrier bag full of purchases.

He eyed her full hands with astonishment

156

and, she thought, some displeasure.

'What on earth have you been buying?'

'Just a few things to make us more comfortable and something to read.'

She pulled out some boiled sweets. 'Want one?' He accepted her peace offering.

Before she knew it, they turned off the main roads. The car bumped along a small track. Darkness surrounded the car, and all she could see outside was the yellow tunnel in front of them made by the car headlights.

'Where are we?'

Rufus stood up in the back, panting in excitement.

'The cottage is just at the end of this lane.' As he spoke, they pulled up behind a small stone building, the rough-hewn stone showing yellowy grey in the headlights.

'Wait here. I'll go and switch the electricity on.' He jumped out of the car and crunched away around the corner into the dark. Rufus made a mournful little moan as his master vanished.

A few minutes later, the cottage lights came on. Nate reappeared to open the back of the car. She could hear the sound of the waves and guessed the sea must be quite near.

Nate hefted the overnight bags from the car. 'Come on. I'll show you round.'

He led the way along a narrow path skirting the back and side of the cottage. The sound of the sea got louder as they rounded the front of the house. Jenni could hear waves crashing onto shingle.

The cottage had a simple layout. When they entered the front door, they stood in a small hall with the stairs leading straight up in front of them. The kitchen/diner lay on one side of the hall and the lounge on the other. Jenni followed Nate up the stairs. Off the tiny landing she discovered two small bedrooms and a bathroom.

Nate dropped her bag on the end of the bed in the bigger of the two rooms.

'This is yours,' he remarked gruffly. 'If you'll unpack all the food, I'll make up the beds and get a fire going in the sitting room.'

Jenni looked about her as Nate left to get the cooler bags into the kitchen and to start kindling the fire. Her room seemed very plain with white-washed walls and a simple pine bed. A small pine wardrobe and table stood against the wall near the window.

She unpacked her things into the wardrobe, then walked downstairs to the kitchen. As she stored the groceries away in the cupboards and the fridge, her spirits started to rise. Rufus dashed in and out of the room, his long tail wagging with joy.

Jenni hummed to herself as she turned on the oven and popped in the homemade lasagna Rose had packed. Next, she turned her attention to the contents of the carrier bags of purchases she had made at the service station.

Nate paused in his unpacking. He could hear Jenni singing as she moved about in the kitchen below. Her light clear voice floated melodiously up the stairs as she sang Christmas carols.

He crossed the landing to make up Jenni's bed with the linen they had brought down with them. Jenni had begun to sing Silent Night, her voice ringing clear and true throughout the house. He dreaded Christmas, the season linked forever in his mind with Cerys and the accident. She had always made a big fuss, throwing parties and buying lavish gifts for all her friends.

Since her death, he had shunned as many of the celebrations as possible, only continuing with the office party and his Santa act because it had been expected of him. He frowned as he smoothed the quilt before going back down to the kitchen.

He stopped in the doorway, not quite

taking in the scene before his eyes. Jenni had her back to him and still warbled away as she bent to attend to the oven. On the scrubbed pine table, set for dinner, stood a mini Christmas tree, decorated with flashing lights, tinsel and a star on the top.

Red scented candles were lit along the welsh dresser. He could smell, along with the supper, the essence of Christmas, pine needles and cinnamon. His mind whirled.

Jenni turned around, the tray of lasagna in her hand. The carol she had been singing died on her lips. She looked at Nate, trying to gauge his reaction.

He hated it, she could tell. He had that frozen, closed expression on his face. Without a word, he closed the door. A second later she heard his feet crunch away across the gravel, walking away from the house into the darkness.

By the time he returned some fifteen minutes later, she had replaced his supper in the oven to keep warm and gone to sit in the lounge by the fire. Jenni took another sip of the glass of red wine she had poured to fortify herself.

'I'm sorry, Jenni.'

She saw the Adam's apple in his throat

move as he swallowed. 'I...'

'Over-reacted?' she supplied.

He had the grace to look sheepish. 'I guess that's the word.'

Her heart raced and tension hung like an invisible thread between them. He looked so tired, she thought, utterly exhausted, as if the battle with his inner demons had pushed even him beyond his strength.

'I'll get your supper. Sit down.'

For once he obeyed her. He sank down onto the low floral covered armchair. She prepared his tray and, topping up her own glass at the same time, poured him a glass of wine too. He accepted the tray without comment and ate in silence. Only the crackle of logs on the hearth and the distant roar of the waves disturbed the peace.

Jenni forced herself to sip slowly at her drink. Inside, her stomach twisted and turned. It took all the courage she possessed to stay in the room with him, gazing into the flames and tasting the mellow roundness of the wine in her glass. Nate finished eating and placed the tray down on the small coffee table that stood at the side of his chair.

'I guess I owe you an explanation.'

Jenni shook her head. 'No, Nate. You don't owe me anything. If you want to tell me, then that's different.'

His eyes, which had been half-closed and hooded in the firelight, snapped open. He took a long pull at the glass of wine in his hand.

'I've never shared this place with anyone before.'

She became conscious of her body stilling, only her pulse raced and her mind worked overtime.

'It's been my refuge, an escape from things. That's why it hit me so hard hearing you singing and seeing the Christmas tree,' he paused and took another sip of wine. 'Since Cerys died, I've dreaded Christmas. If I'm honest, it's too painful. I have the staff party because it's what I've always done. I don't celebrate. I don't shop for gifts.' His voice tailed off. She understood the enormous effort it took to tell her this, to attempt to explain something that she sensed even he didn't fully understand.

'I know.' Suddenly she did know. Jenni had been the one who got the gifts, fetched vouchers for his family, organized cards. 'I just saw that little tree and...' Now she took her turn to share, embarrassed by what she was about to confide. 'I haven't anyone to share Christmas with, no one to tug the other end of a cracker or to see or care if I decorate the house or not. I just wanted to share a little bit of Christmas with you.'

She saw the mixture of emotions in his eyes. Compassion, guilt, and worst of all, pity. She finished her drink, then stood her empty glass down with a clunk.

'If you'll excuse me, I think I'll go to bed, Nate. I'll see you in the morning.' She bolted up the stairs before he had a chance to reply. Before her facade could crumble.

She wasn't sure what had woken her. It had taken her a long time to fall asleep. She had heard Nate go to bed a few hours earlier.

Then she heard Nate's voice; urgent, distressed. She pulled on her dressing gown. She knew all about bad dreams, had suffered many of her own in the past. Jenni guessed dreams of the accident tormented him as he slept.

Jenni opened his bedroom door. She saw him clearly in the moonlight. His chest bare, the duvet slipped half onto the floor as he tossed and turned in the grip of the nightmare.

Instinctively, she crossed to his side to sit on the edge of the bed. The mattress dipped under her weight. Her pulse thundered as

163

loudly as the crashing surf outside the window. She slipped her arms around him and cradled his head on her lap.

'Nate, wake up. It's a bad dream, wake up.'

At first she thought he couldn't hear her, that he had gone so deep she couldn't reach him. Then, to her relief, his eyes flickered open.

'Jenni?' He looked up at her as if he thought she might vanish, as insubstantial as his dream.

'I'm here,' she whispered, stroking the wild curls from his brow.

His skin felt damp with sweat under her fingers. His hand closed over hers, stilling the movement. His other arm slid around her.

'Don't leave me.'

She caressed his cheek, watching with relief as his eyes closed again as he drifted back to sleep. Only then did she prop herself up cautiously on the pillow next to him.

The early morning sound of the seagulls wheeling and screaming over the sea woke her. Jenni realized she was alone.

She listened, hoping Nate might be downstairs, but the house remained silent. She sat up and hugged her knees, trying to decide what to do.

The sitting room and the kitchen were empty, although the fire had been re-laid and a half-drunk cup of coffee stood on the counter in the kitchen. Rufus had gone too. She surmised that Nate must have taken him for a walk. Relief rolled over her and she smiled a little as she acknowledged the fear she had been nursing in her heart. Nate had gone to walk his dog. He hadn't left her.

Jenni looked out of the kitchen window, wondering how far they were from the sea, when to her delight, she discovered the wild front garden ran straight down to the shingle at the head of the small crescent-shaped bay. In the distance, she saw them coming back. Man and dog braced against the stiff breeze which blew in off the sea and whipped the waves into foaming white horses.

A chill ran down her spine as she watched them draw nearer, for Nate's face looked as bleak as the weather. A cold stranger headed back towards her.

CHAPTER TEN

Nate wasn't sure how far he'd walked. It had been one of the hardest things he had ever done in his life, getting out of his bed this morning, leaving Jenni still fast asleep on his pillow. Her soft brunette hair fanned out against the white cotton of the pillowcase.

He reached the top of the cliff and began to walk back towards the cottage. The mobile phone in his pocket vibrated. The number of missed messages took him by surprise as he looked at the phone. He didn't recognize any of the numbers as he scrolled through them. When he hit redial and got the news, he pushed his own concerns to the back of his mind. Whatever happened between him and Jenni, she needed him now.

Jenni busied herself filling the teapot. She didn't want Nate to think she had been looking out for him, waiting for him to come back. Rufus came in first. His tail wagged as he dropped a piece of driftwood at her feet, a pleased expression on his hairy face.

'I've just made some tea, would you like a cup?' Her courage faltered along with her voice when she looked at Nate's face.

'We have to go back.' His words took her by surprise.

'Back?' she echoed.

'Sit down, Jenni.' He pulled out one of the kitchen chairs for her. The gravity in his tone scared her.

'What's the matter? What's happened?'

Nate took the teapot from her and sat down on the chair opposite hers. 'I had a phone call while I was out. The only place you can get reception here is on the cliff. They've been trying to get us since early this morning.'

The blood drained from Jenni's body as the implications of his words began to sink in. 'Something's happened to Tracey?' Her voice came out as a whisper. Nate took her hands in his, his long, clever fingers curled supportively around her hands.

'She's in hospital. The police found her this morning, wandering around the streets.'

Tears sprang unchecked into Jenni's eyes. 'What happened?' She searched Nate's face for answers.

'They wouldn't tell me much because I'm

not family. They said Tracey asked for you.'

Dazed, she tried to take it all in. 'Is she hurt?'

Nate shook his head. 'No, mild hypothermia and shock they said. We'll know more when we get back.' His eyes were dark with sympathy.

'How did they know where to find us?' she asked.

'Tracey told them where you worked. They traced us from there.'

'Oh.' Jenni realized he still held her hands. The warmth of his touch eased the chill in her fingers. Nate's face was somber.

'I'm very sorry, Jenni.' He squeezed her hands.

All the while she cleaned and packed, his words kept going round and round in her mind. What did he feel sorry for? The situation with Tracey? That the holiday had ended before it had begun? Or worse, he felt sorry about confiding in her?

On the drive home, she wanted to ask him what he'd meant, but with every mile that passed, the more Nate appeared to be retreating from her.

By the time they pulled into the hospital car park, Jenni's nerves had disintegrated into tatters. Nate waited with her at the reception desk while they checked which ward Tracey was on. After a brief telephone call, a young policewoman came down to meet them.

'Mr. Mayer, Miss Blake, I'm glad you were able to come home so soon. There's no reason to be unduly alarmed, however.' She gave Jenni a reassuring smile. 'I'm just here to finish taking your mother's statement and to fill you in on the background before you go in to see her. She's been through a dreadful ordeal.'

She led the way to a small side room. When they had been seated and a ward domestic had bought in a tray of tea, the policewoman explained what had happened.

'Your mother was found in a distressed state, Miss Blake, by the beat officer.'

Nate leaned forward. 'I don't know if you're aware of the circumstances, but Jenni hasn't seen her mother since she was a baby.'

'I was given up for adoption. I only traced my mother recently.' Jenni explained. The policewoman's brow cleared.

'Are you aware of her home circumstances?' she asked.

Nate told her everything they knew, including the findings of Mr. Field and the note Jenni had received.

'Was my mother attacked?' Jenni blurted

170

the question. She feared her leaving to go on holiday with Nate had somehow precipitated the event.

The police officer shook her head. 'Not exactly. When the beat officer found her, she was wearing just a thin nightdress. Mr. Clark, Pete, the man she lived with, had lost his temper, which I understand, wasn't unusual. He smashed the house up. Tracey got scared and ran outside, intending to go back in when he had calmed down.' She paused in her narration, her pretty face sober.

'What happened?' Jenni couldn't take her eyes from the young woman's face. She felt glad of Nate's reassuring presence, even though his expression still seemed frozen in a mixture of pity and concern.

'When she thought it was safe, she went back inside. She found Mr. Clark dead. He'd left her a note. In his psychotic state he thought she had gone for good, and the balance of his mind was so disturbed, he killed himself.'

Nate swore softly under his breath. Jenni gasped with horror.

'Your mother was in a state of shock when she was found. She hasn't anyone she could call. She gave us your name as her next of kin.'

Jenni wiped her eyes with the back of her hand.

'I'd like to see her.'

Nate glanced at her. 'Are you sure, Jen?' His voice sounded gruff with concern.

Jenni nodded. 'She needs me, and I want to see her, talk to her.'

The policewoman stood up.

'Do you want me to come with you?' Nate offered.

She looked at his face, seeing his tired eyes and the days' growth of beard he hadn't yet had a chance to shave off. Her heart skipped a beat as she forced herself to shake her head.

'Go home, Nate. You've done enough already.' She knew he must want to be gone. He didn't need to be saddled with her problems now.

At first, she thought he wasn't going to agree, but something in her expression, or maybe the policewoman coming to put her arm around her to support her, convinced him to go. As she let the officer lead her towards her mother's room, she thought her heart would break into a million pieces as she watched the man she loved walk away from her.

The bullets of warm water pelting his skin might have been cleansing his body, but Nate found they did little to clear his mind.

An hour later, his mind still filled with thoughts of Jenni, he gave in and called the ward. The sister informed him Miss Blake had already left. He cursed himself under his breath for having missed her, then jumped in his car and set off for Jenni's flat.

She opened the door. As he stood in front of her, his heart melted at the sight of her weary face. He could have kicked himself. He should have brought her some flowers. 'I called the hospital but they said you'd already left.'

'Tracey needed some rest, so I came home. I just got in.' Jenni's voice sounded totally flat.

'I brought your bag.' He indicated her overnight bag, which rested at his feet. She made no move to invite him in or to pick up the luggage.

'Jenni, are you alright?' He had never seen her look so unhappy.

'I'm fine. I just need a little time to take everything in. I'd appreciate the rest of the week off, Nate, if that's okay. I want to spend some time with Tracey. I'll be there for the dance on Saturday.' She picked up the bag.

Disappointment clawed at him. 'Take as much time as you need. Are you sure you'll be alright for Saturday?'

'I'm sure I'll have things sorted out by then. I'll meet you at the Langstone.' He had been dismissed. She didn't want him around.

'Jenni, promise me if you need anything, anything at all, you'll call me.' If she just gave some sign, some hint then...

She gave him a weak smile. 'I promise. Thanks for everything, Nate. See you Saturday.' The door closed in his face with a click.

Jenni leaned on the back of the closed door. A single tear tickled down her cheek. She wiped it away with a fierce dash of her hand. She would have to be stronger than this if she had to cope with seeing Nate on a daily basis.

The rest of the week passed quickly as she helped Tracey sort out a house move with the housing association, and spent time getting to know her mother better. She soon discovered that beneath her mother's bleached blonde hair and tight clothes beat a generous and kind heart. The more time she spent with her the more easily Jenni could see how so many people had taken advantage of Tracey's good nature.

Nate rang her every night after she had returned from the hospital. He sent flowers for her mother and offered financial assistance. In reply, they chatted about work, the weather, the party. Everything except their feelings. Conversation between them remained brief and punctuated with lengthy pauses. Jenni often hung up after speaking to Nate and wondered why he'd called her.

Saturday morning dawned as one of the bright, crisp, clear winter days that made Jenni want to wrap up and go shopping. She pulled on her new coat and a warm scarf before heading for the high street to browse amongst the Christmas shoppers.

She had started on her way back to the flat when she spotted the dress. She had intended to wear the red one she had worn for the dinner at the hotel, but this one beckoned her from the stand in the window of a new shop just off the high street.

'I suppose there's no harm in trying it on,' she mused to herself. Then noticing the sign announcing 'fabulous opening offers', she decided it must be fate and walked in.

She had felt a little guilty at going to the party and wondered if she should spend the time with Tracey. Her mother, however, had soon stopped that idea.

'Go to your party and enjoy yourself. We've plenty of time to get to know one another again now. You need more pleasure in your life.'

Jenni had been surprised at her mother's statement.

'From everything you've told me, Jenni, you were a good and dutiful daughter to your parents. I don't want you to miss out on things because you feel you have an obligation to me.' Tracey stroked Jenni's cheek. 'I've wanted to see you for so long. I never forgot you.'

Jenni swallowed hard at the sadness on Tracey's face.

'I was so young, just seventeen and your father was the same age. I thought he was wonderful.' She broke off and wiped her heavily made-up eyes with a tissue. 'I didn't know I was pregnant at first. When I found out it was too late to tell him. His family had emigrated to Australia. I was on my own.'

Jenni cried with her, tears coursing down her cheeks as all the questions she had asked herself over the years were answered at last.

'I tried to manage, but after a while I knew I wasn't being fair to you. You deserved much more than I could give you. You were such a good baby, I knew someone else would love you as much as I did, and would give you all the things I couldn't.'

She sighed. 'I tried to choose the best for you, Jenni. I always wondered who you'd look like. Eric, your dad, was so handsome. You're dark haired like him. He was an art student. All the girls hung after him. He used to play guitar in a local band.'

For the first time in her life Jenni felt as if she knew who she truly was as the pieces of the puzzle had all come together at long last.

Jenni took a taxi to the Langstone just after lunch. The hotel had given her and Nate a room each for changing and storage. She dropped her bag on the bed and looked around at the expensive drapes and bed-covers. A few short months ago, she would have been overwhelmed at the chance to stay in such a beautiful place. Nate was booked into the room next to hers. They had been told they could stay the night as guests of the Langstone management.

Jenni checked all the presents on the list and ensured Nate's Santa suit hung ready on a hanger in his room for him to change into, later in the evening. Now she knew how difficult he found the Christmas period, it moved her that he cared about his employees so much that he had continued the company tradition.

Reception phoned Jenni's room just as she stepped out of the bath, to let her know Nate had arrived. She heard him unlock his door as she toweled herself dry with the hotel's luxurious cotton towels. It troubled her that her heart raced and her legs wobbled.

'How am I going to do this?' she whispered to herself as she listened to the faint bumps in the adjoining room. Each time she had spoken to him on the phone, she had stuttered and stammered like a teenager. His conversation had been dry and impersonal, peppered with enough pauses she wondered if he'd call back the next night.

Nate wasn't looking forward to the evening ahead. Lots of people all enjoying themselves, drinking too much, laughing too loud and making fools of themselves under the mistletoe. He scowled at the scarlet Santa suit hanging on the wardrobe door, a neat list of names in Jenni's handwriting pinned to the front.

'I should have hired a Santa.' Even as the

words passed his lips, he knew he couldn't have. His employees looked forward to seeing him dress up and have fun with them once a year. The party was a real tradition. One he knew his staff enjoyed.

The only good thing was that he would have a chance to talk to Jenni at last. If he could just get her alone to discover if he had any kind of chance with her, or if he had simply left it too late.

Jenni added the finishing touches to her hair and stepped back from the full-length mirror. The midnight blue dress fitted her like a glove. The blue chiffon around the top of the bodice softened the line of her bare shoulders and the long slit at the back revealed her long slim legs.

She jumped when a short, peremptory knock rattled her door. After a last look in the mirror and a deep breath, she pulled the door open. Nate waited for her, resplendent in a tuxedo. The combination of his brooding good looks and the formal clothing conspired to render her speechless. Her carefully prepared greeting died in her throat.

His dark blue eyes traveled the length of her body from the tip of her coiffured hair to the bottoms of her spiky heeled shoes.

The intensity of his gaze seemed to scorch the bare skin of her shoulders where the soft velvet left them exposed. He cleared his throat.

'I, er, thought we might have a drink together before everyone arrives. You can fill me in on the running order.' His eyes never left her face. Jenni struggled to make the constricted muscles in her throat function. She cursed herself for behaving like an idiot as she managed to croak out an acceptance.

'In that case, I'd be honored to escort you to the bar.' He proffered her his arm. If he noticed the momentary hesitation before she slipped her arm through his, he didn't comment.

A lone barman polished the glasses ready for the champagne, which waited to greet each guest as they arrived, in the empty bar. Jenni felt too nervous to contemplate alcohol of any sort just yet, so Nate brought a glass of lemonade to where she stood by the picture windows, looking at the gardens which were illuminated by various colored lights.

'It's so pretty out there. Like a little bit of magic.' She spoke without thinking, fascinated by the way the plants and trees assumed new forms when bathed in color.

'It's very pretty in here too, Jenni. *You* look very pretty.'

She felt a rush of heat at the suggestion in his voice. 'Nate, I think it might be best if we go back to the way we were, don't you?' She decided to take the bull by the horns while she had the opportunity for a quiet face-to-face chat with him.

'Best for whom, Jenni?' The anger in his voice startled her. She had been so sure he would be relieved by her suggestion. His eyes blazed blue fire in a face that had paled. 'I don't think it's going to be so easy.'

'It wouldn't work, Nate. We wouldn't work.' Jenni tried to school her voice so she would sound cool and dispassionate, as if she had considered it objectively. She couldn't look at him, because she knew her face would betray her.

'I see.' Nate's voice sounded clipped and icy. 'You've obviously given it a great deal of thought. Perhaps you'd like to explain why.' A muscle pulsed in his cheek and his voice held a bitter edge.

How could she explain her feelings? Nate didn't love her, he felt sorry for her and she wanted, no, needed much more than that from Nate.

She took a deep breath.

181

'Jenni! Are we too early?'

She turned to see a group of girls from the administration office heading towards them. It already looked as if they were in the party mood.

'We'll continue this conversation later, Jenni.'

'I think we've said all there is to say, Nate.'

As she walked across to meet the giggling secretaries, she felt as if her heart had well and truly broken in two.

Nate watched Jenni walk away from him to meet the admin girls who stood by the bar. How had he managed to make such a hash of things? She seemed further away from him now than ever. Jenni asked the bartender to begin serving the champagne. Soon, they all started to laugh and joke together. More of his staff came to join them, and gritting his teeth, Nate crossed the room to do his duty as host.

The party soon got into full swing. Everyone appeared to be having a good time, including Jenni. She made a superb hostess and ensured no one got left to stand alone or with an empty plate or glass. His attention was magnetically attracted to her slim, swaying figure as she moved from group to group.

The one person she didn't want to chat with, it appeared, was him.

Time and again, he caught up with her talking in some group, and as soon as he approached, she disappeared. Now she had been cornered by Mike Walker, who leaned toward her and dangled something that looked a lot like mistletoe over her head.

Nate checked himself from rushing to her side. Perhaps she preferred Mike Walker's company. He watched them closely. Jenni's body language looked uncomfortable. Walker stood much too close. Unable to check himself any longer Nate crossed the room to Jenni's side in a few paces.

'I think it's time the hostess danced with the host, don't you?'

Jenni flushed a delicate pink color. He thought she might be about to argue with him. Mike tucked his mistletoe back inside his jacket pocket.

'If you two don't mind, I'll just go get a drink.' The accountant slipped away, looking anxious to exit the war zone before the missiles started to fly. From the look on Jenni's face, they would all be aimed at Nate.

'What was that about? I can take care of myself,' she asked, crossing her arms.

'I know, but I think it's time you and I

danced together before I go change into Santa and distribute the presents.' Nate held his hand out towards her.

She viewed him with suspicion. 'Maybe I don't feel like dancing.' The band started to play a popular slow ballad.

'Well, I do. Everyone expects it.' He willed her to accept.

Her beautiful eyes flashed fire. 'That's blackmail.'

She took his hand and he led her onto the crowded dance floor. When people saw them coming they clapped and cheered, making a little space. Nate gathered her in his arms. They started to dance to the music. He could feel her standing stiff and ramrod straight in his arms.

'Relax, Jenni, it's just a dance.' He heard the indignant hiss of her breath and took the opportunity to pull her closer. She remained rigid in his grasp, then relaxed a little and leaned into him. Her body felt soft and warm against his. He smelt the faint vanilla perfume she always wore.

'Why are you doing this, Nate?' she murmured against his ear, her voice breathy with an emotion he couldn't define.

'We need to talk. About you and me.' He surprised himself by his choice of words,

184

but he knew he had to make Jenni listen to him. The song ended and he felt her move out of his reach.

'Time for you to be Santa.' She hadn't given him any indication of whether she might be prepared to hear him out or not.

'Promise me we'll talk.'

He noticed her swallow as if nerves had made her throat as dry as his own.

'Alright, but you'd better go and change.' Nate nodded. If Jenni had given him her word he knew she wouldn't break it. He hurried upstairs to change into the Santa suit and collect the gifts. He just hoped he would be able to find the right words.

Jenni watched him go with a troubled heart. What had she let herself in for? Hadn't it been just a few days ago he had told her in this very building *I was in love once.*' She flinched. The words still had the power to hurt her. After everything he had gone through with Cerys, he wasn't looking for the kind of relationship that Jenni knew she wanted. The kind of relationship she deserved. One where she was loved for who *she* was and not some ghostly imitation of another woman.

At last it had ended. The last of the guests

185

had gone. Jenni and Nate remained alone. She felt dead on her feet. The strain of the evening sucked all the emotion out of her, leaving her lifeless and numb. The bar staff remained busy collecting the last of the empty glasses. Jenni felt as flat as the champagne dregs.

Jenni didn't want to talk to him. She felt sure she knew already some of the things he would say. How he could never fall in love with anyone again, and how it might be better if she looked for another post in the New Year.

'I've ordered coffee for us.' Nate came over to where Jenni sat in a small alcove that overlooked the gardens.

'I'm so tired, Nate. I think I'd just like to go to bed.' Jenni wished her heart would stop its painful thumping every time she looked at him. Even dressed as Santa Claus, he was sexy.

He raked his hand irritably through his hair. 'We need to sort things out between the two of us, Jenni.'

'There's nothing to say, Nate.' To her dismay, she burst into tears.

He sank down beside her on the couch. 'We can't turn back the clock, Jenni. Is that what you'd like to do?' His eyes locked with hers.

'I...' Her voice failed her and she shrugged lost in misery. She could see their reflections in the window pane, a tired woman in a blue velvet gown and a handsome man dressed as Santa Claus. Two strangers framed in a gold glow, like the scene on a Christmas card. 'I just can't go on like this, Nate. I don't want to be anyone's second best and I know that's all I will ever be to you.'

She watched the color drain from his face, leaving him pale and ashen in the mellow light of the alcove lamp.

'That's not true, Jenni. After the time we've spent together, you must know that.' His eyes darkened with anguish. 'Is there someone else, Jenni? Does Mike Walker mean something to you?'

'You know he doesn't.' She felt astonished that he could still have any doubts about her feelings for Mike.

'Then what else do I have to do to convince you, Jenni?' His voice shook with suppressed emotion. 'I love you.'

She was desperate to believe him but how could she? 'No, you don't! You loved Cerys, everyone knows that. I'm just Jenni, the mousy girl in your office, remember. The one who gets to go play pool and eat pizza.'

'Cerys is my past, Jenni. You taught me

that.' He rubbed his face. 'I love you, Jenni. You and your silly Christmas tree and lousy flower arranging. I love the way you play pool and walk round a freezing field in the dark with my stupid dog. I love *you.*'

'I'm not right for you, Nate. You need someone like Jo Marchant, someone sophisticated and elegant. I'm not like that.'

He rounded on her, 'Are you listening to anything I'm saying to you? I love you, Jenni. You're worth ten of Jo Marchant any day. Don't you see? Cerys was the one who was the imitation of what love should be about, not you.'

Jenni stared at him, struggling to accept what he had just told her. *Nate loved her.*

'If you don't feel the same way then say so, Jenni. I know I've been an idiot, but over the last few weeks I've finally come to appreciate what love really is. You've shown me that because for me, that person is you.'

The anguished note in his voice betrayed the depth of his feelings.

'Oh, Nate.' She slipped her arms around his neck. She thought of all the things he'd done for her, the risks he'd taken. The truth had been there in front of her face and her own self-doubt had blinded her.

'I love you, Jennifer Blake.' He slipped

from the edge of the sofa to kneel at her feet. 'I love you, and I'm asking you if you'll do me the honor of becoming my wife.'

She leaned forward and kissed him tenderly on the lips. A fierce hunger swept through her at the brief contact, setting her heart soaring free from the iron bands of pain which had tormented her for so long. 'I love you, Nate, and I would be honored to accept.'

'Of course, there is one thing,' she added.

A shadow passed over his face, 'What's that?'

'Well, I will have to make sure it's you inside that suit. I don't want to end up as Mrs. Claus by mistake,' she said. 'It's not every day a girl gets a proposal from Santa.'

His eyes sparked at her words, 'If you marry me, Jenni, I promise you can check as many times as you like.' He swept her into his arms and sealed his promise with a kiss that took her breath away.

'You're the only one I want, Nate. Now and for the rest of our lives,' she promised.

The publishers hope that this book has given you enjoyable reading. Large Print Books are especially designed to be as easy to see and hold as possible. If you wish a complete list of our books please ask at your local library or write directly to:

Magna Large Print Books
Magna House, Long Preston,
Skipton, North Yorkshire.
BD23 4ND

This Large Print Book, for people
who cannot read normal print,
is published under the auspices of

THE ULVERSCROFT FOUNDATION